TRAPPED IN A LIE

"You've been telling everyone that I went through your things last week at your apartment!" Alexis said. "You know that story is a lie. I would never do a thing like that. You owe me a big apology."

"*I* owe *you* an apology! That's a laugh!" Laura shrieked. "You went through *my* things."

"I didn't!" cried Alexis. "That's the last thing I'd do to a friend—or someone I *thought* was my friend."

Laura flinched for an instant. Alexis had just called her a friend. In that moment Laura hated herself. How had she gotten into this horrible, ugly mess? she wondered.

She glanced at the faces around her. They were all riveted on her, wondering what she would say next. In a split second she formed her strategy. Pointing to Alexis's Wakeman charm bracelet, she said in a deadly serious voice. "You stole that from me. That's my bracelet, Alexis Duvall, and you stole it."

THE FABULOUS FIVE

Laura's Secret

BETSY HAYNES

A BANTAM SKYLARK BOOK®
NEW YORK · TORONTO · LONDON · SYNDEY · AUCKLAND

RL 5, 009–012

LAURA'S SECRET
A Bantam Skylark Book / September 1991

ISBN 0-553-15871-6

Published simultaneously in the United States and Canada

*Bantam Books are published by Bantam Books, a division of Bantam Double-
day Dell Publishing Group, Inc. Its trademark, consisting of the words
"Bantam Books" and the portrayal of a rooster, is Registered in U.S. Patent
and Trademark Office and in other countries. Marca Registrada. Bantam
Books, 666 Fifth Avenue, New York, New York 10103.*

PRINTED IN THE UNITED STATES OF AMERICA

CWO   0 9 8 7 6 5 4 3 2 1

Laura's Secret

CHAPTER

1

"*Oh, no!*" Laura McCall wailed. "I can't believe it! This is terrible!" She glared at her reflection in the mirror and pounded her fist on the edge of the bath-room sink.

"What is it? What's wrong?" her father's voice called from his bedroom.

Laura moaned. "Oh, nothing. My life is just ruined, that's all," she said.

She stared at the red splotch on her new white blouse, the blouse that made her figure look so great and went so well with her stonewashed jeans. Thirty seconds ago it had been perfect. Now it had a large blob of liquid blush smeared into it, right in front.

"I'll *never* get this out," Laura muttered to her mirror image.

There was a tap on the bathroom door.

"Come in!" Laura said angrily, rubbing the spot with her finger.

"What's the trouble, babe?" Laura's father asked, pushing the door open and poking his head inside. With their reflections side by side in the mirror, it was easy to see that they were father and daughter. Both were tall and slender with sandy blond hair; Laura's was styled in a long braid that started at the top of her head and fell over one shoulder.

"My new blouse! I just ruined it!" Laura wailed. "I spilled this blush on it, and it's probably on there permanently!"

"Can't you just wash it out?" Walker McCall asked.

He strode over to the neatly-folded stack of clean washcloths on the bathroom vanity, picked up the cloth on top, and ran it under the water.

"Are you kidding, Daddy!" Laura cried. "You'll set the stain for *sure* if you put cold water on it!"

She grabbed the washcloth from her dad.

Didn't men know *anything*?

Her father certainly didn't. Oh, sure, he was a great dad, and she loved him very much. But he had no idea how to take care of clothes or keep the apartment clean, and he joked that if there hadn't been ready-made baby food, he would have been feeding Laura hamburgers and pizza when she was an infant.

She should be used to it by now, though. Laura had lived with her father ever since she was a baby. Her mother, Clare, had left them and gone to New York City not long after Laura was born, saying that she wasn't cut out for motherhood. Clare had become a successful fashion designer, and Laura rarely saw or spoke to her.

Her father had hired a woman named Mrs. Skinner to take care of the apartment when Laura was small, but now that Laura was older, most of the responsibility fell on her shoulders. She did the cleaning, shopped for the groceries, cooked most of the meals, and washed the clothes—except for her father's shirts, which went to the dry cleaner.

Lately things had been even worse than usual. Her father was in fierce competition for a huge promotion at work, and he had become an absolute *bear* to live with, always growling at her about something or other. Do this! Do that! She knew that he was under a lot of pressure, but it was driving her berserk.

Walker McCall shrugged. "Guess I can't help you with the blouse. Besides, you know more about this stuff than I do." He glanced at his watch. "I've gotta go, babe. I have an important meeting with one of my biggest clients this morning. I've got to impress my boss all I can before that promotion is decided." He checked his reflection in the mirror and straightened his tie. "Oh, by the way, would you iron my blue shirt with the pinstripes tonight? I've got to pitch a new client tomorrow, and there isn't time to send it to the cleaners."

Laura let out an exasperated sigh. "Okay, okay," she said.

Mr. McCall leaned over and kissed his daughter's cheek. "Go find yourself a new blouse," he told her. "I'll buy it for you. Say, be sure to clean up the apartment before school, okay? It's a wreck. You and your friends left a mess in the living room yesterday."

Laura didn't speak, but nodded, her lips pressed tightly together in frustration.

Her father smiled fondly in the mirror at his daughter. "What would I do without my chief cook and bottle washer?" he said, chuckling. "See you tonight, hon."

When Laura heard the apartment door close a moment later, she let out a scream. "*I can't stand it anymore! I'm his slave! It isn't fair!*"

She stomped into her bedroom, tore off the blouse, and threw it on her bed. She opened her closet and began flipping through the expensive, stylish clothes hanging there.

"This one's not the right color. I'll freeze in this one. This one isn't ironed. Nope, nope, nope." Tears gathered in her eyes. "What am I going to *wear* today? This is terrible! The new blouse would have been awesome!"

She leaned against her closet door and imagined her classmates' reaction to that blouse. All the guys would have turned to watch her walking down the hall, and the girls would have been green with envy. Laura smiled. She enjoyed that, seeing the other girls watch her, admire her, wishing they were Laura McCall.

Ha! she thought. What a riot. If only they knew. They're wishing themselves into slavery.

But they never would know. She would see to that. After all, why did they admire her in the first place? They thought she had it made, living with her bachelor dad, getting chauffeured in his bright red Maserati, wearing gorgeous clothes, and entertaining kids in her apartment without a parent around to bother them.

Laura sighed and turned back to her closet. "Guess I'm slumming today," she murmured, picking out one of her least expensive blouses. "At least it's clean and ironed. And it doesn't have a big red stain on it." She looked closer. Well, there *were* a couple of little wrinkles up near the collar, because her closet was too small and everything in it was smashed together, but the blouse would have to do as it was. There was no time to iron it.

She wondered if she'd be able to find another blouse

like the one she had ruined. She had to admit that it was nice of her father to offer to buy her another one, and she certainly intended to take him up on it. She'd have to rush down to Tanninger's department store right after school.

Laura finished dressing and managed to get the kitchen cleaned up before she had to leave for school.

She found her friends, the other three girls that made up The Fantastic Foursome, waiting for her at the corner of the school building. Funny Hawthorne, leaning against the brick wall, stood up straight when she saw Laura coming.

"Here comes Laura the Beautiful!" Funny cried, grinning. She began to sing to the tune of "America the Beautiful": "Oh, beau-ti-ful for spa-cious eyes, for am-ber waves of hair—"

"Hi," Laura said, a big smile spreading over her face. She loved Funny's song. Of course Funny could be a ditz sometimes, but she was fun to have around. She got such a kick out of everything.

"Hey, I didn't get to finish," Funny protested, giggling.

"Yeah," chimed in Tammy Lucero. "I was waiting to see how you were going to rhyme the 'hair' line."

"Whoa," Melissa McConnell said, eyeing Laura critically. "I haven't seen you wear *that* blouse in ages!"

"So what's wrong with it?" Laura replied defensively.

Melissa shrugged. "Nothing, really. You just don't usually wear your older clothes to school. I mean, it's okay. It's just a little wrinkled."

Laura felt her face getting red. She wasn't used to criticism from other kids, especially her friends. Of course, Melissa always looks so perfect herself! thought Laura. And she looks down her nose at anyone who doesn't.

She bit her lower lip and thought about Tammy's motor mouth. Tammy meant well, but with her love of gossip, the blouse incident would be all over school by the end of the day. All the kids would be smirking behind Laura's back. Some of them were so envious of her, they seemed to *live* for the moment Laura McCall slipped up.

She felt her face grow hotter. She couldn't have that happen.

"Well," she improvised quickly, "I'd be wearing a really gorgeous white blouse today if—if the *maid* hadn't ruined it!"

Funny let out a gasp. "The *maid*?" Her eyes grew wide. "You have a maid?"

"I didn't know you had a maid!" chimed in Tammy.

Melissa's eyes narrowed. "Since when?"

Laura shrugged and lowered her eyes to avoid Melissa's gaze. "Oh, since a couple of weeks ago, when my dad got a big promotion. I guess I just forgot to tell you."

"Wow!" said Funny. "That's awesome! I wish we had a maid at our house!"

Laura gave a quiet sigh of relief. Sure it was a lie, but at least her friends weren't criticizing how she looked anymore. In fact, they looked positively jealous.

"Does your maid live with you?" asked Funny.

"No," Laura answered. "She comes in every morning after I leave for school."

"What does she do?" Tammy asked.

"Oh, she picks my clothes up off the floor, washes the breakfast dishes, cleans the apartment, that kind of thing," Laura replied casually.

"Wow!" said Funny.

"And then she makes dinner for Dad and me," Laura added. Her story was getting better by the second!

"You're kidding!" exclaimed Tammy, slapping her forehead with the heel of her hand. "What does she cook?"

"Whatever we order," Laura said airily. She was enjoying watching her friends' faces. Even Melissa was buying the story, although she was holding back her enthusiasm the way she always did. "Sometimes we have her make lasagna and a salad, or maybe we'll order enchiladas and Spanish rice."

"Yum!" Tammy licked her lips.

This is really going to get around, Laura thought happily. Tammy will spread it all over school! She imagined all the kids talking about her in reverent whispers, murmuring "maid" and pointing to her as she passed by. It would be so great!

"So what's her name?" asked Melissa, joining the conversation again.

Laura blinked in surprise. "Her name? Uh, well—it's—Chantal."

"Chantal?" asked Funny.

"Yes," said Laura. "She's French."

Tammy's mouth dropped open. "A *French maid*?"

"Wow!" Funny kept repeating. "Wow!"

Tammy grinned broadly. "I should have guessed that that Maserati dad of yours would hire a French maid."

"Does she prance around your apartment in a short, little skirt and high heels, and use a feather duster?" Funny asked, trying to hold back the giggles.

"And say *'oui, oui'* all the time?' asked Tammy.

Laura laughed. "No, not exactly. But Chantal *is* beautiful."

"Wow!" Funny said again.

"And what's most important," Laura continued, plastering her most sincere expression on her face, "she's absolutely *devoted* to Dad and me. You know, it really is hard to get good help these days."

"So how did she ruin the blouse?" Melissa asked.

"The bl—oh, yeah, the blouse!" Laura said. She'd almost forgotten how her story had gotten started in the first place. "Well, Chantal was hand-washing it for

me—it's a very fine, delicate fabric—and she accidentally knocked some blusher on it that I had left sitting
on the sink."

"Oh, that's too bad," said Funny.

"Well, Chantal felt just *terrible* about it," Laura told
her. "She offered to buy me a new blouse, but Dad and
I decided not to make her do that. After all, it was just
an accident."

"Gosh, that was nice of you guys," said Funny.

"Yeah, pretty generous, if you ask me," agreed
Tammy.

"Well, she's starting to seem like part of the family,"
said Laura.

Funny shook her head, grinning. "Boy, Laura. You
really have it made. You really, REALLY have it
made!"

Laura smiled. *If they only knew!*

CHAPTER

2

"Sit here, Laura." Tammy patted the spot next to her at the lunch table.

Tammy, Funny, and Melissa were already seated at The Fantastic Foursome's regular table in the cafeteria. The girls were eyeing her with more than the usual amount of interest. That maid story had sure paid off!

"Hello, everyone," Laura said, sliding her tray onto the table and sitting down with them.

"I'm surprised you don't have Chantal pack you a fantastic lunch to bring to school," Funny commented. "These school lunches are so gross!"

"You said it," grumbled Tammy. "Goulash! The absolutely *ickiest* food ever invented."

Funny giggled. "Come on, Tammy, you can take it."

Then turning to Laura, she added, "Yeah, Laura, why don't you?"

"Oh," Laura said, smiling and waving her hand, dismissing the idea. "Well, she comes after I leave for school. Besides, Chantal works hard enough making us dinner and cleaning up the apartment. I guess I can force down school food to give her a break."

"Let me tell you, Laura," Tammy said. "I'd ask my maid to fix me peanut butter and jelly rather than face the school's goulash."

"So why don't you make your *own* peanut butter and jelly sandwich then?" asked Melissa.

"Too much bother," Tammy replied.

Funny giggled again. "But not for the maid, right?" The girls laughed.

"I can't imagine having a maid," Tammy said dreamily. "I mean, not having to clean up your room or take your turn washing dishes . . ." She took a bite of a carrot stick.

"What do you do with all that spare time that the rest of us don't have?" Melissa asked.

Laura grinned. "I have fun."

The others groaned.

"You already had it easy, not having a mother breathing down your neck," Melissa said.

Laura's smile faded a little. Melissa had no idea how *hard* it was not having a mother. Laura had no one to ask about blush stains on her blouse, or the best way to deal with boys, or . . .

The faces of her friends faded as she remembered last year when she got her period for the first time. What a disaster! She hadn't had any of the supplies she needed, she didn't know *what* to do, and she was too embarrassed to ask her dad about it. She ended up scribbling down the name of a brand of pads she'd read about in *Seventeen* magazine and taking it to the drugstore. She'd paced up and down the aisles for fifteen minutes before she found a female clerk to show her piece of paper to. When she'd brought her purchase home, she'd headed straight for her room and locked the door.

Safely alone, she'd read every word on the box and figured out for herself how the pads were used. If only she had had a mother to talk to. It would have been so much easier!

". . . and my mother drives me nuts!" Melissa's voice floated back into Laura's consciousness. "She's always making me baby-sit for my little sister, even if I already have plans of my own."

"What I like about your setup, Laura, is that you can have kids over to your apartment any time you want to," said Tammy. "Nobody else I know gets to have friends over without parents around."

Laura smiled. "Yeah, I like that, too."

I'd still rather have a mother, though, she thought.

"So," Laura said to the group. "You want to come over tomorrow after school? The next day's Saturday, so your parents won't be able to say you have to go straight home and do your homework."

Tammy rolled her eyes. "Boy, do I hear *that* a lot."

"Yeah," agreed Funny. "Let's go to your place."

"Great," Tammy said.

Laura looked at Melissa. "Sure," Melissa answered. "Sounds good to me."

Laura gazed toward the ceiling. "Let's see," she said slowly. "I'll ask Alexis Duvall, Marcie Bee, Sara Sawyer, and Lisa Snow to come over, too. In fact, I'll have Chantal make some special snacks. How does that sound?"

Chantal sure does come in handy, Laura thought, smiling to herself. Of course that little extra lie was going to mean a lot of extra work tonight, baking cookies and other goodies, but boy, were her friends impressed!

"Great," said Tammy. "And we'll gab our brains out!"

Funny giggled. "You do that *already*, Tammy."

Tammy stuck out her tongue playfully, and the girls laughed.

"We'll *be* there," The Fantastic Foursome said in unison.

*   *   *

Laura sat at the kitchen table and stared at the frozen dinners in front of her. *If only we really had a maid*, she thought, *we'd be having something totally awesome for dinner.*

She put her hand on her abdomen. Terrific. Cramps starting. Her period had begun just this afternoon, so Laura should have known cramps couldn't be far behind. What rotten timing. She had so much work to do tonight! She had to get the apartment as spic and span as a maid would, bake cookies and brownies, and—

"Don't forget I need that shirt ironed, hon," her dad said, dabbing his mouth with a napkin.

And the shirt!

It was a good thing she'd already finished her homework.

The dull pain in her abdomen increased a little, and she leaned toward the table and sighed heavily.

"You okay, babe?" her dad asked.

"Yeah," answered Laura. How do you tell your dad you have cramps? It wouldn't be hard to tell your mother.

"You look a little pale."

"Oh, I'm okay," Laura assured him.

He reached over and felt her forehead. "You don't seem to have a fever," he offered. "But maybe you're coming down with something. Why don't you go to bed a little early tonight?"

Fat chance!

"Maybe," Laura said.

If only she could talk to her dad! She'd seen a medication advertised on TV that was supposed to help with cramps. She wished she could ask her father to go to the drugstore and buy some for her.

Laura got up from the table and carried her plate to the sink. When she heard her father stroll into the living room to watch television, she breathed a deep sigh. Then she cleaned up the kitchen and got out the mixing bowl, flour, sugar, chocolate chips, and other ingredients she needed. She turned the oven on to 350 degrees.

By now the cramps were awfully uncomfortable. She crossed the living room and walked into the bathroom. Behind the closed door she took a couple of aspirin. That should help, she thought.

When she left the bathroom and reentered the living room, her father looked up from the TV. "Laura?"

"Yeah?"

"You really aren't feeling well, are you?" he asked, frowning with concern.

"Well, not really great, I guess," answered Laura.

"What's the problem?" pressed her father.

Dare she tell him? Had any girl on the face of the earth ever told her father she was having cramps?

"Well—"

"What's wrong, sweetie?" he asked.

"Oh." She shrugged, pretending it was nothing. "Just some, uh—cramps, I guess." She said the last three words very quickly and very softly.

Her father's eyes darted away, and Laura could have sworn he turned a little pink. Was he embarrassed? She turned quickly and fled into the kitchen.

Why did I tell him, she scolded herself. *I'm an IDIOT!*

She furiously tossed ingredients into the bowl. Turning the mixer on high speed, she worked the spatula around the inside of the bowl.

"Hon?"

She suddenly realized that her father was right beside her.

"What?" she said loudly, partly to be heard over the mixer, partly out of nervousness.

"I thought this might help."

He held up a bottle of milk of magnesia. A *LAXATIVE*! Her father held it up near his face as if he were selling it on a TV commercial.

If Laura hadn't been so embarrassed, she would have exploded with laughter. *Her father was hopeless!*

"Thanks, Dad," she murmured, her cheeks hotter than the oven. She grabbed the bottle, put it down on the table, and stared at the floor.

"Uh, well," her father said, rocking nervously from foot to foot. "I brought a lot of work home from the office. I guess I'd better get at it."

"Okay," Laura replied. *The sooner, the better.*

Her dad left the kitchen, and Laura shook her head. *Men! They're pitiful. It's amazing how dumb they can be about women.*

She started to laugh quietly. Then she thought of the way her father looked, holding up that silly bottle of milk of magnesia, and she laughed harder. A laxative for menstrual cramps! What a riot!

She finished baking the cookies, then started a batch of brownies. When the brownies were finally in the oven, she hauled out the ironing board and plugged in the iron, pressing and spray-starching her dad's dress shirt.

"Here's your shirt, Dad," she said when she'd finished, standing in the doorway to his room and holding up the hanger so he could see what a great job she had done.

He looked up from the pile of papers on his desk. "Terrific. Hang it in my closet, will you, hon?"

Laura heaved a sigh of fatigue, trudged into her father's room, and hung up the shirt. She was getting awfully tired. And she still had the cleaning to do.

She took the brownies out of the oven, pulled the vacuum out of the front closet, and vacuumed the living room and the hallway.

As she was putting the vacuum away, her dad stuck his head out of his bedroom. "I'm turning in early," he told her. "I want to be sharp for that presentation tomorrow."

"Okay," Laura said. "Good-night."

Going to bed sounds good to me, too, she thought. I'll finish up the kitchen and do the rest of the cleaning in the morning before I leave for school.

She headed for her room and her soft, comfortable bed, daydreaming about having her friends over the next afternoon. She couldn't wait to see their reactions to the goodies that "Chantal" had slaved over!

CHAPTER

3

"*H*ere we are, guys," Laura announced, grinning. She unlocked the apartment door and led Melissa and Tammy inside. "Let's *party*!"

"Does anyone know where Funny is?" asked Tammy. "I thought she was supposed to be here, too."

Laura shrugged. "She wasn't at her locker, but she knows we're having a party today. I'm sure she'll be here in a few minutes."

Tammy plopped down on the living room couch. "Hey, Laura, when are Alexis, Marcie, Sara, and Lisa coming?"

"Any minute," Laura answered. "They said they'd be here right after school. What do you guys want to drink?"

Tammy followed her into the kitchen. "Chantal really keeps this place clean. Not even a spoon in the sink."

Laura smiled. She nearly hadn't gotten the cleaning done this morning. She'd been so tired last night that she'd forgotten to set her clock radio. She'd awakened ten minutes later than usual this morning, and she'd still had dusting to do, dishes to wash, and her bathroom to clean.

She'd managed to finish everything by skipping breakfast. Then, just as she was about to head out the door for school, she'd spotted a big pile of dirty clothes in one corner of her bedroom. She couldn't let her friends see that. After all, Chantal kept things spotless. She'd grabbed the pile of laundry and pitched it into her father's bedroom, slamming the door. She would gather it up again and do the wash after everybody left.

Now Laura peeled the aluminum foil off the pan of brownies and the platter of cookies.

"Wow!" said Tammy. "Those look wonderful." She took a cookie off the top of the platter and tasted it. "They're incredible." Then she raised an eyebrow and said in her most sophisticated voice. "Send my compliments to your maid."

Laura laughed. "Sure. Why don't you take them into the living room, and I'll bring the drinks."

There was a knock at the door, and Melissa ran to

answer it as Laura entered the room with a tray of drinks.

"Hi, guys!" Tammy cried. "Come on in. We've got the place to ourselves, as usual, and Laura's maid baked some terrific stuff."

"Maid?" asked Alexis, walking into the apartment. "I didn't know you and your dad had a maid, Laura."

"They sure do," said Tammy. "Look at this place— squeaky clean. And taste these yummy cookies."

The girls settled themselves around the living room. Laura took drink orders from the new arrivals and hurried back into the kitchen. While she was pouring the soda, she listened to the conversation in the other room.

"Laura lives a life of luxury, you know that?" said Tammy. "What a setup!"

"Yeah," agreed Melissa. "This is living."

"I thought only movie stars had maids," Lisa added.

Alexis spoke up. "We have a maid."

"Really?" three voices chorused.

Laura frowned. *Alexis would have a maid! And of course she's going to tell everybody about it.*

"If I had a maid," commented Tammy, "I could forget about chores and concentrate on more important things—like BOYS!"

"Yeah!" cried everyone.

Laura laughed in spite of herself and opened a bag of

potato chips. She dumped half of the bag into a large ceramic bowl, put it on the tray with the drinks, and carried it out to the living room just as the doorbell rang again.

"Must be Funny," she said, setting the tray on the table and hurrying to the door.

Funny was breathless as she came in. "Wow, what a bummer," she said.

"What happened?" asked Laura. "Where have you been?"

Funny shrugged off her jacket and looked at the others with exasperation. "Miss Dickinson kept me after class to talk to me about my giggling in English class."

"Your giggling!" hooted Tammy. "It's about time someone mentioned it. You giggle all the time."

"So what finally got you into trouble?" asked Laura.

"Well, you know how dramatic Miss Dickinson can get sometimes when she's reading a poem out loud. You know, how she swoops around the front of the room as if she were on stage?"

The others nodded.

"Well, today she was doing that, and Joel Murphy ducked down behind Clarence Marshall and started imitating her. It was a scream. I just couldn't help it. I started laughing, and naturally Miss Dickinson saw me."

"Did she see Joel, too?" asked Lisa.

Funny shook her head. "And I didn't dare tell her, because she would want to know what he was doing that was so funny."

"Well, you can laugh all you want to here," Laura told her, chuckling at Funny's predicament. "Sit down and have something to eat."

"Hey, did you hear that Keith Masterson sat with Shawnie Pendergast at the game last weekend?" asked Tammy. She grinned. "I bet Beth Barry was furious."

Laura laughed. "Serves Beth right. She's such a show-off. Did you ever see anybody wear such bizarre clothes?"

Funny giggled. "I kind of like her style, though," she said, cocking an eyebrow. "She's got guts!"

Laura snorted. "You'd never catch *me* wearing some of the combinations she comes up with."

"I saw Keith sitting with Shawnie," said Marcie, "but I happen to know that Shawnie was just saving a place for Beth. Shawnie even sat with Beth and Keith for the rest of the game. Besides, doesn't Shawnie date Craig Meachem?"

Tammy grinned impishly. "So what? Shawnie might've *pretended* she was saving a seat for Beth. But what she really wanted was to be near Keith. She was flirting with him like you wouldn't believe."

The girls continued to gossip about kids at school while they devoured cookies, brownies, and chips, and drank soda.

"Hey, did you get some new charms for your Wakeman bracelet?" Tammy asked Funny.

Funny nodded, holding up her wrist and shaking it a little to make the charms clink together softly. "My mom gave me the one spelling *Wakeman* in cursive letters for my birthday last week, and Melissa gave me this jukebox."

"I love those Wakeman charm bracelets," said Tammy. "I'm going to ask for one for Christmas."

Laura was pleased that everyone seemed to be having a good time. Of course that was her reputation—she had great gossip parties, with *no parents around*.

"What time is it, Laura?" asked Sara.

Laura glanced at her watch. "Four-thirty."

"Rats! My mom is picking me up in fifteen minutes," said Sara. "You know, she's starting to drive me nuts!"

"Tell me about it." Melissa rolled her eyes. "My mother is like a drill sergeant."

"Man, Laura," said Lisa, "I hope you know how lucky you are."

"Right," Laura replied, forcing some enthusiasm into her voice. "I've got it pretty great."

Alexis smiled. "I guess I'm pretty lucky then. My mother and I get along pretty well."

"Really?" asked Funny in amazement. "Don't you ever argue with her?"

Alexis shrugged. "I guess we argue sometimes, but

it's never very serious. Basically, I think of her as a friend. I can tell her just about anything."

Laura felt a wave of envy wash over her. It must be great to have a mother you can tell your secrets to.

"Gee, your mother must be a very understanding person," Funny said.

Alexis nodded. "She is. She still remembers what it was like to be in junior high."

"Back in the dark ages." Funny chuckled.

"Right," Alexis agreed, and laughed. "She had some of the same problems with boys that I sometimes have."

Tammy's eyes nearly popped out of her head. "You talk to your mom about *boys*?"

"Sure," Alexis answered. "She's saved me from doing some pretty stupid things."

"Wow." Funny shook her head in amazement.

Alexis turned to Laura. "Can I use your bathroom?"

"Sure," said Laura. "Through my bedroom and to the right."

Laura watched Alexis as she headed down the hall, and she wished for a moment that she could trade places with her. Not only did the Duvall family have plenty of money, but also Alexis was popular, and now it turned out she had a terrific mother. What more could any girl ask for?

Laura hopped up, went out to the kitchen, and brought back the bag of potato chips. She emptied the rest of the chips into the ceramic bowl on the coffee table. "Anybody want more cookies?" she asked. "Or brownies?"

"I thought you'd never ask," said Sara. "I could eat a *ton* of those terrific cookies."

Laura headed for the kitchen, piled more cookies on the platter and returned to the living room.

". . . well, I heard that Mrs. Lemane had a face-lift," Tammy was saying.

The rest of the girls roared with laughter.

"Are you kidding?" asked Funny.

"Well, just *look* at her sometime," Tammy insisted.

"But I don't take French," Lisa protested.

"Okay, well, next time you see her in the hall," Tammy suggested, "go up to her and say something, and look at her face."

Lisa frowned. "But what should I say?"

"Just make up something," said Tammy. "The point is to get really close so you can examine her. Just look at the skin around her eyes. It looks really *tight*."

The girls howled again.

Laura looked around the room. Alexis was still gone. Uh-oh, thought Laura with a sudden stab of panic. What if I forgot to put out towels or something a maid would *never* forget to do? Jumping up, she headed down the hall and into her bedroom. She stopped short in the doorway.

Alexis was standing still next to Laura's bureau, reading a scrap of paper that was taped to the mirror.

Laura gulped. Her father always taped messages on her mirror when he was angry with her, and lately, since he was on edge about the promotion, he was angry with her a lot. She moved closer to the bureau and cringed as she read the note over Alexis's shoulder.

Laura,
  What's the big idea of throwing YOUR dirty laundry all over MY bedroom? Is this some kind of new teenage rebellion? All I ask is that you keep the apartment reasonably clean, and I come home for lunch and find this! We'll talk about it tonight.
                              Dad

Laura froze.

CHAPTER

4

Laura's stomach lurched as she reread the part about keeping the apartment clean. Alexis turned to look at Laura, but didn't speak.

What could Laura say? Her mind spun wildly until she suddenly came up with an idea.

"Oh, Dad!" she scoffed, pretending to be impatient with her father. "It's the maid's day off, see, and I was just playing a little joke on him—"

"But you said the maid cleaned the apartment and made all those snacks for us," said Alexis.

"Well, she did, see," Laura fumbled, "but she did that yesterday. And I was supposed to straighten things up this morning so that she won't have too much to do when she gets back. Actually, that was when I decided to play this joke," Laura rushed on, hoping Alexis wouldn't see how flustered she was becoming, "but my dad has absolutely *no* sense of humor."

Alexis looked skeptical.

She doesn't believe me! Laura thought. I have to do something fast.

"So what were you doing looking at private notes on my mirror, anyway?" Laura demanded, her voice rising with panic and anger. "I said you could use my bathroom, not snoop around my room!"

Alexis took a small step backward. "I'm sorry," she said. "I've always liked the way you decorate your room, so I just stopped to admire it for a moment."

"Yeah, right!" Laura snapped, reaching for the note and ripping it to pieces. "That's a pretty lame excuse, Alexis."

"Really," Alexis insisted, obviously surprised by Laura's outburst. "I'm sorry, Laura." She paused and looked Laura in the eyes. "I won't tell anyone about the note on your mirror. Honest."

Laura bit her lower lip. It was clear that Alexis still didn't believe her.

Pulling herself up to her full height, Laura shouted, "You're a snoop, Alexis Duvall! You had no right to read my personal notes!"

"I said I'm sorry," Alexis said evenly. Her face was turning red with anger. "I don't owe you any more than an apology!"

Alexis stormed out of the bedroom and down the hall. Laura followed closely, terrified that she would tell the others about the note.

Instead, Alexis grabbed her jacket off the couch and stalked out of the apartment without a word to anyone. The others watched, their eyes wide with surprise. Lisa, Sara, and Marcie said quick thank yous to Laura and left, too.

Probably to run after Alexis and find out what happened, Laura thought angrily.

"Wow, what happened in there between you and Alexis?" asked Tammy.

"Yeah," said Melissa. "We could hear you yelling clear down the hall."

What am I going to say? thought Laura. They're my best friends, but I can't let them find out that I made up the maid story. What would they think? Besides, Tammy would spread it all over school.

"I found out Alexis is a *snoop*, that's what happened!"

Funny wrinkled her nose. "What are you talking about?"

"She was looking at my stuff!" Laura said indignantly.

"So?" Tammy asked. "What's the big deal?"

Laura raised her eyebrows. "I mean, she was going through my things!"

"Going through your things?" echoed Funny. "What do you mean? What exactly was she doing?"

A signal went off in Laura's head. *STOP! Don't say any more!*

"Let's just forget it," snapped Laura. "I just want to forget that it ever happened."

"Come on, Laura," Tammy urged. "We won't tell anybody."

Funny and Melissa each shot Tammy a suspicious look.

"I *won't*!" Tammy insisted. Melissa rolled her eyes.

"I don't want to talk about it anymore," Laura said. "And I want you three to promise me that you won't tell anybody what happened here today."

Funny shrugged. "Laura, we don't *know* what happened here today."

"Well, just forget it then," Laura repeated.

"Okay already," Melissa said. "Come on, you guys. Let's go. I think the party's over."

"See you all later," Laura said, wishing desperately that she could get things back to the way they were before she discovered Alexis in her room.

"Yeah, see ya," said Funny.

The girls gathered their things and left. Laura watched the door close behind them and began pacing around the room, her mind filled with anger and worry. What if Alexis blabbed about the note on her mirror? It would be all over school that Laura was a liar.

She sighed. She had always liked Sara, Lisa, Marcie, and Alexis. And she knew they had liked her, too. No, she thought. It was more than that. They thought I was someone special. Really special. But what will happen now, if Alexis tells everybody about the note, and they all turn against me? I won't have anything. No mother to talk to and no friends, just a dad who doesn't understand anything, and tons of housework. She felt tears spilling down her cheeks, but she jerked upright and wiped them away with the back of her hand. This was no time to get weepy, she told herself sternly. What she needed was a plan.

Well, she knew one thing: The Fantastic Foursome would stick by her. At least they'd *better*, if they wanted to remain her friends!

Laura saw the rest of The Fantastic Foursome leaning against the building when she arrived at school on Monday. She waved. Funny waved back.

Why didn't Melissa or Tammy wave? she wondered. Are they mad because I wouldn't tell them what happened with Alexis? Then she stopped in her tracks. *Had Alexis told them about the note already?*

As Laura slowly approached her friends, Funny smiled and called, "Hi, Laura."

She forced a smile. "Hi, everybody."

"I hate Mondays," said Melissa. "Five whole days of drudgery before we get any fun."

Tammy sighed. "I know what you mean. I hate Mondays, too."

They didn't even say hi to me, thought Laura.

"Yeah," agreed Funny. "Did you all get your math homework done?"

"Barely," answered Tammy.

"It was a hard assignment," commented Melissa.

"What a week," said Funny. "I've got three tests before Friday! Can you believe it?"

Laura stood silently and listened to the conversation. They're leaving me out, she thought. They aren't even talking to me!

The bell rang, and the girls pushed off the side of the building and trudged toward the school. Walking through the front door, Melissa waved and headed off in the direction of her locker.

Why didn't she say, "See you at lunch?" Laura wondered.

"Oh, there's Samantha," pointed out Tammy. "I have to hear how her date with Josh went on Saturday night. See you guys later," she said, rushing down the hall.

Just then Beth Barry and Jana Morgan walked by. Beth saw Laura, ducked her head, and whispered something to Jana. Jana laughed, and the girls continued on to their lockers.

"Did you see that?" Laura demanded.

"No, what?" asked Funny.

"Beth saw me and smirked and then said something to Jana," Laura replied hotly. "Then Jana laughed."

"Yeah?" said Funny.

"Yeah!"

Funny looked puzzled.

"They were talking about *me*!" Laura insisted.

"You're imagining things," Funny said, frowning. "They're best friends, remember? Beth says nutty things all the time."

"Yeah, right," Laura answered sarcastically.

Funny grinned. "You're just being paranoid. Hey, see you at lunch."

"Thanks for all your sympathy," Laura grumbled, but Funny didn't hear. She had aleady disappeared into the crowd moving down the hall.

"Well, this day is really getting off to a great start," Laura muttered as she headed for her locker. "I can hardly wait to see what happens next."

The morning moved at a snail's pace. Laura watched the faces of the kids in her classes, but everyone seemed to be ignoring her the way her best friends had. Was Funny right? she wondered. Am I paranoid? Or is everyone snubbing me?

By lunchtime she was convinced that the whole school had heard the details of her blow-up with Alexis. She stopped in the bathroom just before lunch and glimpsed her reflection in the mirror. Her shoulders were stooped, the corners of her mouth were turned down, and her eyes looked tired and angry.

Laura was shocked. Usually she looked terrific. She straightened her shoulders, held up her head, and looked herself squarely in the eyes.

You're not going to let them get you down, she told herself silently. You're going to act as if there is absolutely nothing wrong. Then when kids see you, they'll think that Alexis is just making up the story. You'll look so *together*, no one will believe in a million years that you lied about having a maid!

Laura felt better as she hurried to the cafeteria, went through the hot-lunch line, and slid into her ususal seat next to Tammy.

"Say, Laura," Tammy said, shooting a meaningful glance at Melissa and Funny, "remember when you said that Alexis was going through your things?"

Laura blinked in surprise. "Yeah?" she said, feeling suddenly defensive.

"What *really* happened?" asked Tammy, a small smile playing on her lips. "We've been talking about it, and we want to know."

"I told you I didn't want to discuss it," Laura said, trying to keep her voice even. That old, familiar panic sensation was returning to her chest.

Tammy looked offended. "We just wondered. After all, we are your best friends."

Laura breathed a sigh of impatience. "And I don't

want you saying anything to anybody, either. Do you get me?"

Tammy shrugged. "Okay, okay," she replied.

Laura picked at her lunch and thought about the situation. Now what if Tammy starts a rumor about Alexis going through my things? I don't want that to happen. Alexis has always been my friend.

"Speak of the devil." Melissa nudged Laura. "Guess who just walked into the cafeteria."

Laura turned to look. Sure enough, Alexis was carrying a tray and walking across the room. She saw someone she knew, smiled, and headed toward the left side of the cafeteria.

"Look. She's sitting down at The Fabulous Five's table," said Tammy.

"Yeah," Funny said. "They sit together at Bumpers sometimes, too."

Just great, thought Laura. Of all the times for her to be sitting with my worst enemies.

Laura kept an eye on the table, watching while Alexis, Beth, and Jana talked together. Alexis was doing the talking, and suddenly Beth and Jana broke out laughing. Then Melanie Edwards leaned into the conversation to say something, and the whole group laughed louder than ever.

"Melanie is such a ditz," Laura remarked sourly.

Funny giggled. "I think she's a riot. She's the most boy-crazy girl I've ever known."

Laura continued to watch Alexis out of the corner of her eye. Was she telling them the maid story right now? Once during lunch Alexis glanced over toward Laura, and their eyes met. Laura was about to smile at her, but before she could force the corners of her mouth to turn up, Alexis looked away.

Well, I tried! Laura thought. She sat up straight and tossed her long braid over her shoulder. I tried to show her I wasn't mad anymore, but she wouldn't even look at me. I have to get out of here before I explode. She stood up.

Tammy looked at her in surprise.

"Are you finished?" she asked. "You hardly touched your sloppy joe."

"I'm going to study hall," Laura said. Then she added a little lie. "I've got to study for my math test."

"Well, could I have your sandwich?" asked Tammy. "I'm still hungry."

Laura picked up her sloppy joe, plopped it on Tammy's plate, and started off to the garbage can to dump the rest of her lunch.

"Hey, I just realized something," Tammy called after her. "I'm in your math class. We don't have a test."

CHAPTER

5

*W*hen Laura came home from school, she picked up around the apartment. Next she got chicken out of the refrigerator, dipped the pieces in milk, rolled them in flour, and lined them up in the bottom of a glass baking pan. Then she popped them into the oven.

All the time she was thinking about Alexis. What a total disaster it would be if she broke her promise and told everybody about their argument. Especially, thought Laura, if gossip-of-the-world Tammy blabbed Laura's story about Alexis going through her things.

It was all her father's fault. If he hadn't put that stupid note on her mirror, none of this would have ever happened. Sure, he had an excuse for being extra crabby lately. He was worried about that promotion. If

41

he got it, he would be the youngest vice president in the company. "Big deal!" grumbled Laura. "It's ruining my entire life."

Laura went into her bedroom and flopped onto the bed. She turned on her radio and stared at the ceiling. The music was soothing to her nerves. Her adrenaline had been pumping like crazy all day, and now she was exhausted. Her eyelids drooped, and she sank deeper into her pillow. Thoughts of Alexis and Tammy and her father melted together into a dreamy darkness.

"Laura!" her father called from the living room.

Laura's eyes flew open. "What?" she mumbled.

An instant later Walker McCall was standing in the doorway to her bedroom. "Fall asleep?"

Laura sat up slowly and stretched. "Guess so," she said.

"When's supper, hon?" he asked. "I'm meeting some of the guys from the office at the bowling alley in an hour."

Laura looked at the clock. "Chicken should be ready in a few minutes. I'll fix a salad and some instant rice. It'll be ready in a jiffy."

"Good," her father said. "I'm starved."

Laura got up and scooted into the kitchen. She stopped in front of the stove and gasped. "Oh, no!"

"What?"

Laura opened the oven door and stared at the pan of raw chicken sitting inside. It was stone cold. She had been feeling so frustrated over Alexis that she had left the kitchen without turning the oven on.

"What's the matter?" he asked from over her shoulder.

Laura turned red. "The chicken . . . it's not cooked. I must have forgotten to turn on the oven."

"*What!*" Her father gave her a look of utter astonishment. "Do you mean to say that you just left it sitting in a cold oven while you fell asleep in your room?"

Laura stared at the floor. "Um-hm."

"Great," he muttered. "Just great."

"I'm sorry, Dad. I could make you a sandwich."

He sighed heavily. "What kind of sandwich?"

She threw open the refrigerator door and frantically looked over each shelf and in each drawer. Eeek! she thought. No cheese. No luncheon meat. No veggies. No fruit. No *anything*.

Laura turned slowly to her father. "Peanut butter and jelly?" she asked hopefully.

"Are you kidding?" he asked in exasperation.

"It'll only take an hour for the chicken to cook. In fact, if I turn the oven a little higher than the recipe calls for, it'll probably cook faster," she offered. "Why don't you sit down and watch TV? Before you know it, dinner will be ready."

"I *told* you I'm going bowling in an hour," said her father, his voice rising in anger. "Not only that, my biggest competition for that promotion is on the other team, and he's a terrific bowler. I need to be on top of my game."

Laura bit her lip and stared at the floor. "I'm sorry," she whispered. There it was again, she thought. That promotion. Pressure or not, did he have to blame her for everything? She hadn't *meant* to goof up his dinner.

Her father looked at the ceiling, trying to regain his calm.

"I shouldn't have yelled at you like that," he said finally. "I'm sorry. I know you didn't mess up dinner on purpose."

"That's okay," Laura said. "I mean, I'm sorry. I just forgot."

"Yeah, and sometimes I forget that you're still a kid. Still my little girl," apologized her father, looking at her tenderly. "Listen," he added, suddenly brightening. "Come here, will you? There's something I want to talk to you about." He took her hand and led her into the living room. "Sit down."

Laura sat on the edge of the couch, while her dad sank into the big, upholstered chair next to her. What's this all about? she wondered.

"Listen, I'm going to ask you to do me a special favor."

Laura eyed her father suspiciously. "What?" she asked.

"I'm going to bring home a . . . lady I want you to meet," he said.

Laura blinked in surprise. "A girlfriend?"

He cleared his throat self-consciously. "Well, yes, I guess you could call Trudy a girlfriend."

"Trudy?" she asked, grinning slyly.

"Yes," her father said. "That's her name. Trudy Dwyer."

"What does this Trudy Dwyer look like?" Laura wanted to know. The argument about the chicken seemed far away now.

Her father stared off into the distance and said, "She's a terrific woman. Beautiful. You're going to like her." Then he looked back at Laura. "And I want the place looking very nice, and I want you on your best behavior. Get it?"

Laura nodded.

"Trudy is going to come here tomorrow evening," he continued. "We're going out for dinner and a movie. But I wanted her to meet you first—I've told her what a great kid you are. You don't have to dress up or anything, but be sure to wear something nice." He thought for a moment. "How about that yellow dress?"

"Yellow dress?" she echoed.

"You know, the one you wore to your cousin Annie's wedding last spring."

Laura wrinkled her nose. "That's old. It's not flattering anymore, either." To herself, she said, This will have to be a really great outfit. I can't have my father's date outshine me!

"Of course it's a flattering dress," her father argued. "You look like my little girl in that dress. The white lace collar is great with your hair."

Laura rolled her eyes. "I think I'll wear my new black skirt with the pink silk blouse."

"I don't remember that outfit." Her father paused. "But if it looks nice, wear it."

Laura grinned. She was eager to meet her father's new girlfriend. Usually she didn't get to meet his dates. Best of all, he seemed to have forgotten all about the raw chicken in the oven. She was off the hook.

"I'm going to change clothes," her father said. "Then I'm going out for a hamburger on my way to the bowling alley. See you around ten-thirty. Do you want me to bring you anything?"

Laura smiled. "No thanks, Daddy."

The next morning Laura spotted her friends at their usual place at the corner of the school building. But someone was standing with them. Alexis! She was wearing her blue denim jacket with the hand-painted Western scene on the back. It had to be Alexis. No one else at Wakeman had a jacket like that. Laura narrowed her eyes. Alexis was talking to the girls.

And she looked *mad*!

Tammy looked up and saw Laura coming. She must have warned Alexis, because Alexis whirled around as if she were confronting an enemy. Laura slowed. She knew that the moment she had dreaded had finally arrived.

Her mind ticked off the possibilities, and in the next instant she knew what she would do. She would take the offensive.

"What's the matter with *you*, Duvall?" Laura asked nastily. Maybe she could intimidate Alexis into backing down.

"You know very well, Laura McCall," Alexis countered. She didn't look as if she would back down at all. Her face was bright red with anger.

"I have no idea," said Laura airily, trying to make it sound as if she couldn't care less, either.

"I've heard all the rumors you've been spreading about me," Alexis said.

"What rumors? I haven't said anything about you."

"Oh, yes, you have. You've been telling everyone that I went through your things last week at your apartment!" Alexis replied.

"And where did you hear that?" challenged Laura. She threw Tammy an angry glare. Tammy's face fell, and she shrank back.

"I heard it from Sara Sawyer, who got it from *your friend* Tammy," Alexis told her. "But since then, I've heard it from lots of kids."

"Really?" Laura asked sarcastically.

Laura noticed the color drain from Tammy's face. Good. She's terrified! Laura thought.

"You know that story is a lie," Alexis said, her face hardened with fury. "I would never do a thing like that! You owe me a big apology!"

There was no turning back. Laura had created this horrible situation; now she had no choice but to see it through. Backing down was unthinkable! She would lose face in front of the whole school. A large group of kids had already formed around them. The Fabulous Five—minus Christie Winchell, who had moved with her family to England—were standing behind Alexis and off to the side. Even worse, Laura could see out of the corner of one eye that a group of seventh-grade boys had appeared and were watching from a few yards away. Randy Kirwan, Keith Masterson, and even Shane Arrington were there. What would they think of her if she admitted she had lied?

All of these thoughts flashed through Laura's mind in a millisecond. *Stand up for yourself, or you're dead!* a frantic voice cried out in her head.

"*I* owe *you* an apology! That's a laugh!" Laura shrieked. "You went through *my* things!"

"I didn't!" cried Alexis. "That's the last thing I'd do to a friend—or—or someone I thought was my friend!"

Laura flinched for an instant. Alexis had just called her a friend. At that moment Laura hated herself.

Hated herself and what she'd just done to Alexis. How had she gotten into this horrible, ugly mess? she wondered.

She glanced at the faces around her. They were all riveted on her, waiting to see what she would say next.

Laura was trapped.

She glanced down and in a split second formed her strategy. Pointing to Alexis's Wakeman charm bracelet, she said in a deadly serious voice, "You *stole* that from me. That's my bracelet, Alexis Duvall, and you stole it."

CHAPTER

6

"*What!*" Alexis cried, her voice rising an octave above its normal pitch. "This is *my* bracelet, Laura McCall! I can't believe it! Now you're calling me a thief!"

The kids surrounding the two girls gasped at Laura's accusation. Laura heard murmurs of disbelief run through the crowd. But suddenly another sound caught her attention. Giggling! She spun around angrily just as Funny clamped a hand over her mouth and looked at Laura in wide-eyed panic.

Dropping the hand, Funny whispered so softly that only Laura could hear, "I'm sorry. I really didn't mean to laugh. It's just that sometimes when I get nervous—"

"You can't say that about Alexis!" someone called

from the back of the crowd, drawing Laura's attention away from Funny.

"Alexis is as honest as anybody I know!" cried Beth Barry.

Of course The Fabulous Five are going to stick up for Alexis, Laura thought.

But they weren't the only ones taking Alexis's side. Obviously there were a lot of kids who respected Alexis enough to stand up for her.

Laura felt a twinge of envy creep over her. It must be nice to have such loyal friends. The Fantastic Four-some sure weren't being too vocal in her defense. And Funny's outburst of laughing was outrageous. Sure, she giggled a lot of times when she shouldn't, but how could she laugh *now*?

"That's my charm bracelet, Alexis, and you know it," Laura repeated, forcing herself to keep her voice under control. She had to forget about Funny for the time being and concentrate on the problem at hand.

I'll let Alexis rant and rave while I stay calm and cool, Laura decided. *She'll look hysterical*.

Katie Shannon, who was standing with the rest of The Fabulous Five, stepped forward and placed a hand on Alexis's shoulder.

"You're accusing Alexis of stealing," Katie said to Laura. "That's a very serious charge."

"You bet it is!" Laura spat out the words. "And it's also none of your business, Shannon! So butt out."

"Well, all I have to say is that if you're going to ac-
cuse Alexis of stealing, you'd better be able to prove
it," Katie replied.

"She *can't* prove it," Alexis said. "It's a lie."

Laura glanced around at the faces surrounding her.
Everyone was watching her closely. Would she be able
to pull this off? she asked herself.

Laura thought fast. "I *can* prove it," she countered.
"Here, give the bracelet to me."

Alexis angrily tore off her bracelet and thrust it at
Laura.

Laura's pulse was racing as she turned it over slowly
in her hand. Some of the kids moved in closer to look
over her shoulder. The charm bracelets, which were
being sold by the school's Spirit Club to raise money
for new cheerleading uniforms, were designed to de-
pict various elements of life at Wakeman Junior High.
On Alexis's bracelet there was a tepee charm, repre-
senting *The Wigwam*, Wakeman's yearbook; the name
Wakeman spelled out in cursive letters; a bumper car for
Bumpers, the kids' favorite hangout; and a comb and
mirror. Laura bit her lower lip, hoping no one would
notice that this bracelet did not contain a megaphone,
which members of the cheerleading squad, like Laura,
wore.

Suddenly she spotted a tiny scratch on the tepee
charm. "There!" she said triumphantly. "There's your
proof." She shoved the bracelet back into Alexis's hand.

"What?" demanded Alexis.

"The scratch on the tepee," Laura said. "I accidentally scratched it with a piece of silverware one day when I was washing dishes."

Alexis looked closely at the tepee charm. Then she looked back up at Laura and narrowed her eyes. "That must have happened before you got your *maid*," she said.

Laura felt her face heating up. *Was Alexis going to break her promise and tell about the note on the mirror?*

"I remember when that happened." Tammy rushed to Laura's defense. "I was at your apartment that day. Remember?"

Laura stared at Tammy. She was obviously trying to make up for blabbing Laura's rumor about Alexis all over school.

"That's right," Laura said. "Sure I remember."

Tammy turned to Melissa and Funny. "Don't you remember that day? When Laura was washing dishes and she scratched her bracelet? She almost came unglued." Tammy glanced hopefully back and forth between Melissa and Funny.

"No," Melissa answered flatly. "I don't."

"I'm sorry." Funny turned her eyes away from Laura. "But I just don't remember it, either."

"Well, I still have a witness," Laura said to Alexis. "And I guess you don't have anything." She grabbed the bracelet back again and slipped it into her pocket. "Not even a charm bracelet."

"Okay," Alexis retorted, her face red with fury. "Okay, Laura, since you have branded me a thief in front of everyone here, I'm sure you won't mind if I tell them what I found taped to your dresser mirror that afternoon at your apartment, will you?"

Laura's heart jumped into her throat, but she refused to let Alexis see that she was scared. She lifted her chin and said sarcastically, "No, Alexis, I don't mind. What *did* you find taped to my dresser mirror that afternoon at my apartment?"

Alexis looked around at the crowd of kids and directed her answer to them. She spoke softly, without anger, as if she were telling a simple fact.

"There was a note from Laura's father," Alexis began. "He was angry because Laura had thrown dirty laundry into his bedroom when he had asked her to clean up the apartment."

No one spoke.

"You see," Alexis continued, "Laura had been bragging to everyone that she had a maid who waited on her and her father hand and foot, cleaning up the apartment, cooking them dinner, everything."

Alexis turned and faced Laura. "I think Laura was embarrassed that I found that note. It proved she was lying about the maid to impress everyone. So"—Laura could hear the anger returning to Alexis's voice—"she accused me of going through her things and stealing her bracelet!"

Laura lifted her chin even higher and looked at Alexis icily. "You can make up all kinds of lies to hide the truth, Alexis, but it won't work. It's your word against mine, and I have the proof, the scratched bracelet."

Laura looked around at Tammy, Melissa, and Funny. "Come on, let's go," she said. "This is boring me."

She turned and walked away with Tammy right behind her. Out of the corner of her eye she could see Melissa and Funny hesitating. *What's the matter with them?* Laura panicked. *Aren't they coming?*

Finally Funny shrugged and said, "Well, I have to get to my locker. I left my history notes there last night, and I have to cram for class today."

"I'll go with you," Melissa said quickly, hurrying after Funny.

The nerve of those two! Laura thought, stalking away angrily. They don't believe me. Some friends they are.

"That was awful!" Tammy said, skipping to keep up with Laura's furious pace. "All those kids siding with Alexis and standing around gawking at you both, as if it was some kind of show."

"Oh, shut up, Tammy," Laura snapped, stopping to stare Tammy in the face. "You started it all."

Tammy's face turned white. "I did?"

"Of course you did!" Laura cried. "You blabbed all over school about Alexis going through my things. I *told* you I didn't want anybody to know about that."

"Well," Tammy replied, her voice quivering, "I only told Sara Sawyer, but I told her that she absolutely could not tell *anyone* about it. You just can't trust Sara. She's the biggest blabbermouth I've ever known!"

"Next to you," said Laura. She whirled around and stomped off, leaving Tammy standing alone at the corner of the school building.

The rest of the morning was terrible. Word of Laura's face-off with Alexis was all over school, and everyone was taking sides. Most kids seemed to think that Alexis couldn't possibly be a thief. But what bothered Laura most was Melissa and Funny. Not only had Funny acted like a ditz by giggling at the absolutely worst moment, but even worse, neither of them had defended her in front of the crowd. Deep down, Laura knew that they weren't any more convinced that Alexis was a thief than were most of the other kids.

So what! Laura slammed down her hand so hard on her book that kids around her in history class stared. Whose friends are they, anyway? They're part of The Fantastic Foursome, of which I am the leader, and they owe me their loyalty!

Laura sighed. It had been a long time since she had made them *prove* their loyalty. She had always liked the feeling of control it gave her when the three of them did extra special things to convince her of their friendship. Like the time she ordered them to do all her homework for an entire week. Or when she made them spy on The Fabulous Five to see if they were gossiping about her. With all the orders she had to take at home, sometimes it was the only part of her life where she felt in control.

Laura couldn't possibly concentrate on schoolwork that morning. She stared off into the distance instead, turning the whole mess over and over in her mind and examining every detail.

She knew she was getting in deeper, but what choice did she have? If she admitted she'd made up the story about Alexis stealing her bracelet, she'd become the laughingstock of Wakeman Junior High. Anyway, it was Alexis's word against hers. Laura would just have to ride it out. But it sure was going to be a bumpy ride.

At lunch Laura was amazed that not one of The Fantastic Foursome mentioned Alexis or the bracelet. Instead they exchanged worried glances when they thought she wasn't looking. They're chicken, she thought angrily. They don't believe me, but they don't have the nerve to say it. By the time the dismissal bell rang at the end of the day, Laura couldn't stand it any longer. She had to do something to get her friends back in line. She called a meeting of The Fantastic Foursome at her locker.

"I know what you're all thinking," she began.

The other three girls glanced at each other, confirming Laura's suspicions. She plunged right in.

"You're wondering about the bracelet," she said.

None of the girls spoke, although she waited a moment in case someone wanted to rush to her defense.

Laura cleared her throat. "I can't prove what I said about Alexis taking my bracelet. And I can't prove that I scratched the charm washing dishes."

She looked at her three best friends. They were looking back at her expectantly. They obviously wanted to believe her—but they still weren't sure.

Laura began to cry. All the frustration and guilt she had been feeling the entire morning gave way to tears. "I just can't understand why you guys don't believe me," she sobbed, her face wet with tears. "You're my best friends, and you won't even defend me."

She was aware of the change in her friends the moment she started to cry. The doubt on Funny's face immediately disappeared, and Melissa's eyes filled with sympathetic tears.

Tammy rushed forward and threw her arms around Laura. "Oh, Laura," she exclaimed, "this is all my fault! Me and my big mouth! I feel so awful!"

Funny put a hand on Laura's arm. "I've never seen you cry before, Laura," she said softly. "I'm sorry I doubted you, even for a moment."

"Me, too," Melissa added, squeezing Laura's shoulder. "We should have known better. We're The Fantastic Foursome! We stick together through thick and thin."

Laura sniffed and pulled a tissue out of her pocket.

"Thanks," she said, smiling weakly through her tears. "I knew you guys wouldn't let me down."

Even though it took crying to do it! Laura thought triumphantly.

Still, she felt better.

CHAPTER

7

*L*aura put the finishing touches on her makeup and stepped back from the bathroom mirror. She smiled a little and nodded approvingly.

Old Trudy will have to look pretty terrific to top me tonight, Laura thought.

Her hair had come out just right this morning after she'd washed it, blown it dry, and braided it, starting at the top of her head. Not a loose strand anywhere.

And she felt as great as she looked. The rest of The Fantastic Foursome were loyal to her again, and now she was going to meet her dad's new girlfriend.

Trudy Dwyer. Hmmm, mused Laura. An okay name. How about Trudy McCall? Eeeek! That sounded weird! Laura wondered if Trudy had ever tried out that name. Did Trudy want to marry her dad? More important, how did her dad feel about marrying Trudy?

Laura sank onto her bed and stared at the wall. What would it be like to have a stepmother? She giggled as a picture of Cinderella and her wicked stepmother flashed into her mind. Actually, she reasoned, it might be nice to have another woman in the house. She could do all my chores. And I could talk to her, about girl things. Laura smiled. Of course it depended on the woman. If she wanted to be my friend, that would be wonderful, Laura thought. But if she started acting like my friends' mothers, always telling me what to do and putting restrictions on my freedom, that would be horrible.

Laura glanced again at her reflection in the mirror. She saw the frown on her face and immediately wiped it off. She was worrying about nothing, she told herself. Her dad wasn't *marrying* Trudy tonight, just *going out* with her. She could handle that.

Laura stood up and straightened her black miniskirt. It fit her like a glove. The pink silk blouse clung in just the right places and made her figure look better than ever.

Laura unbuttoned one more button on the front of her blouse. Perfect, she thought. Trudy was going to see that she had plenty of competition for attention at the McCall house.

She went to her jewelry box and took out the gold necklace that her father had given her on her last birthday. It had a cultured pearl hanging from it, and looked very expensive, even though it probably wasn't. She put it on and admired the overall effect.

She was ready for Trudy!

She checked her watch. Her father would be home any minute for a quick shower and change. Then he'd go pick up Trudy. Sure enough, she heard the front door open.

"Laura?" her father called out.

"Hi, Daddy," she answered.

"Remember about tonight?" he said from the living room. "I'm bringing Trudy home for a few minutes to meet you. Are you ready?"

"I remember," said Laura. She hurried in to greet him.

Her father glanced up from the pile of mail he was going through. His expression changed from nearly blank to horrified.

"Why are you dressed like *that*?" he demanded, staring at her.

"Like what?" Laura asked, surprised. She knew she looked terrific.

"Like—like *that*!" he sputtered. "All painted up, with that short skirt! And button up that blouse! What do you think you're doing?"

"What do you mean?" Laura wailed. "I've been working on myself for over an hour."

"That outfit is unacceptable," Mr. McCall insisted, striding across the living room and into Laura's room.

Laura followed her father. "What's wrong with it?" she demanded.

"It's . . . it's just all wrong," he said. He opened his daughter's closet and began flipping through the clothes. He stopped at the yellow dress.

"I think I look . . . nice," Laura said. Nice! That was an understatement. She looked fantastic!

"This is what I asked you to wear," he said patiently. "*This* looks like my little girl, Laura."

"But I'm *not* your little girl anymore. I've grown up, Daddy. Haven't you noticed?"

"You may think you're grown up, Laura, but you're only in seventh grade," he said. "Now, I want you to look like the young lady that you are. And I want you to be very nice to Trudy when she gets here. Got it?"

"That dress is ridiculous!" Laura cried. "Look at all that silly lace. It's totally babyish!"

Walker gazed at his daughter a moment. "Well, you're still my baby," he told her, "no matter what you think. Now, no arguments." He thrust the dress toward her.

Laura let out an exasperated, "Aghhhhhhhh!" and snatched it from her father. She stalked into the bathroom and slammed the door.

*   *   *

An hour later Laura sat on the living room couch dressed in the yellow dress, glumly watching television. Her father had left to pick up Trudy half an hour ago. They were due any minute.

"I look so incredibly stupid in this dress," Laura grumbled to herself. "I look like Pollyanna."

She sat up straight. *Pollyanna! Why not?* Her dad wanted a sweet little girl, and that was just what he was going to get.

Laura laughed and hopped up from the couch. She ran into the kitchen, threw open the freezer door, and pulled out a plastic container of chocolate chip cookies, left over from her fateful after-school party last week. She put a dozen cookies on a plate and set it on the coffee table. Next she ran to the hall closet and pulled out a box filled with wrapping paper and ribbons.

She rummaged through the ribbons and came up with a large yellow one, which she cut into two pieces. Quickly, she unbraided her hair and rearranged it into two ponytails. Then she tied a ribbon on each side.

Laura checked herself in the bathroom mirror and giggled. She looked seven years old! "Perfect!" she said, squealing with glee.

She ran to her bureau and pulled out a pair of short, white socks. She put them on and then put her flats on top.

Just then she heard her father's key in the lock and the front door open. Her dad and Trudy were here!

She took a final look in the mirror. "Like a little kid going to a birthday party!" she whispered, giggling.

"Laura?" her dad called out. "Laura, we're home. Come and meet Trudy."

Laura took a deep breath and *skipped* out into the living room.

"Hi, Daddy!" she sang, plastering a big, Shirley Temple smile on her face. "I'm *so* glad you're home!"

Her father's face went pale. "What the—"

"Would you like some cookies?" Laura asked. She skipped over to the coffee table and picked up the plate, extending it toward Trudy. "I made them myself."

Trudy glanced sideways at Mr. McCall as if to say, "Is this kid for real?" But she didn't open her mouth.

"Uh, well," her father said, his face turning red, "Trudy, this is my daughter, Laura. Laura, this is Trudy."

Laura looked Trudy up and down. At her super-fashionable, short, curly haircut; at her leather jacket, slightly open to reveal a low-cut silk blouse and leather slacks.

Trudy extended her hand to Laura, and jangles of bracelets sounded from her slender wrists.

"Hi, Laura," she said.

Laura took Trudy's hand, then dipped in a little curtsey.

"Pleased to meet you," Laura responded, smiling

her sweetest smile. "And, oh, I really like your outfit, Miss Dwyer. It's so . . . so *feminine*." She turned to her father. "Don't you think so, Daddy? Don't you think Trudy looks nice?"

"Well, yes, it's—" Her father stopped in midsentence. His eyes got big, and he turned back to Laura, looking at her sternly. "Oh, I see what's going on here."

Trudy turned to Mr. McCall and gave him a nudge. "Then will you let me in on it? This doesn't seem like the daughter you described."

He cleared his throat. "Laura has gone to great lengths here to make a point."

Trudy looked interested. "Oh? What point is that?"

Mr. McCall looked at Laura, who smiled at him with sweet innocence. He rolled his eyes. "Oh, brother," he mumbled, and Laura stifled a giggle.

"Laura and I had a discussion about what she would wear to meet you tonight," he explained.

Trudy gazed at Laura in surprise. "And you wanted her to dress like *that*?"

Laura's father let out a heavy sigh of defeat and collapsed on the couch. "I just wanted you to see Laura in pretty, feminine clothes."

"I'm his baby," Laura added wryly. She sat down next to her father and rested her hand on his shoulder.

Trudy's eyebrows shot up. "Just how old are you, Laura?" she asked, sitting down on the other side of Mr. McCall.

"Thirteen. I wanted to wear my black skirt and silk blouse."

"Sounds nice," said Trudy.

"*Short* black skirt and *unbuttoned* blouse," her father elaborated.

"Oh." Trudy nodded. "I see why your dad wanted you to wear the yellow dress instead."

Mr. McCall sighed again. "How about meeting me halfway, Laura?"

"Sure," agreed Laura. "Anything's better than what I'm wearing now."

"I'll accept the short skirt—I guess that's the fashion now—if you'll keep that blouse buttoned up," he said.

Laura grinned. "Deal."

Her father nodded. "Good."

Laura put out her hand to Trudy. "Hey, thanks. You're okay."

"Oh, yeah?" Trudy said, grinning. "Well, you're okay, too, Laura."

"Thanks." Laura sank back into the cushions on the couch. "It's such a relief."

"What's a relief?" asked Trudy.

"That you're dressed that way," she answered. "It's good to know that my dad has taste after all."

CHAPTER

8

"*Laura McCall, I have something to say to you!*"

Laura was walking down the hall with Tammy, Funny, and Melissa after school the next day when a voice stopped her in her tracks. She knew immediately whose it was.

Laura took a deep breath, as if she were trying very hard to be patient. "Is there a problem, Alexis? What is it this time?"

Already some kids in the hall had stopped to hear what would certainly be another terrific argument between the two girls.

"Yesterday you said you had proof that I was a thief," Alexis said.

"I do," Laura replied.

"Yeah, right, that little scratch," Alexis said scornfully.

"That proves the bracelet's mine," Laura insisted.

"Well, I'm going to give you the chance to prove something else," Alexis told her.

"What's that?"

"Prove that you're not a liar," Alexis answered.

The crowd around them was getting bigger. Laura threw Funny a warning look as she spotted The Fabulous Five on one side and Shane Arrington, Paul Smoke, and Dekeisha Adams on the other side. She wished Shane wasn't there. He was the cutest boy in seventh grade, and his presence made her nervous.

Now she looked back at Alexis, who was staring at her, her eyes filled with anger.

"Prove I'm not a liar?" asked Laura. "What do you mean?"

"Prove that you have a maid," said Alexis. "If you can, then everyone will know that you're not a liar!"

Laura gulped.

"But if you can't prove it," Alexis went on, "then they'll know that you invented the maid story to impress everybody and that you lied about my stealing your bracelet."

Laura heard a murmur run through the crowd. Everybody was obviously waiting for her answer.

"I'd prove it if I could," Laura announced, trying to sound confident, "but the maid comes in the mornings when we're all at school." Then she had an idea. "I could have her write you a note."

Alexis laughed sarcastically. "Oh, that would be great proof! After you wrote the note yourself."

Laughter rippled from the kids surrounding them.

That was a stupid mistake, Laura realized. She caught a glimpse of her three best friends standing stiffly beside her, silent as usual.

"Okay," Laura said boldly. "Then why don't you skip school with me—any day you choose—and come to my apartment? You can meet the maid yourself."

There were more murmurs in the crowd.

Laura looked around at the kids. "In fact, any of you who want to can come," she invited. "I'll prove I have a maid!"

She wondered briefly what she would do if anyone agreed to come to her apartment to see the maid. She searched the faces. They looked impressed with her offer, but no one seemed ready to skip school. That was good. Her courage was growing.

Laura looked directly at Alexis. "Come on, Duvall," she challenged. "How about tomorrow? Come to my apartment!"

Alexis's eyes narrowed. "You know I don't skip school, Laura."

Laura shrugged. "Too bad. I could have proved to you once and for all—"

"What's your maid's name?" Alexis interrupted.

"Chantal," Laura said. "She's French."

"Chantal?" Alexis asked. "What's her last name?"

Laura's mind raced. "Uh, DuBois. Chantal DuBois, if it's any of your business."

"Interesting," Alexis said thoughtfully. "And where does this Chantal live?"

"Why do you want to know that?" Laura asked carefully.

"Well," Alexis answered. "I just thought we could find her and clear this up, once and for all."

"Find her?" Laura asked in a small voice.

"Sure," explained Alexis. "There are only two employment agencies in town that represent maids."

"Oh?" asked Laura, her legs feeling weak.

"Well, since we have a maid," Alexis went on, "I asked my parents for the names of both agencies. Now I can call them and ask about a Chantal DuBois. I'll see if they know her."

"Oh," said Laura, grabbing for the first idea that came to mind, "well, that wouldn't help you, anyway. My dad got her through a private ad in the paper."

Alexis smiled. She wasn't defeated. "Well, let's just look in the phone book. There couldn't be more than one Chantal DuBois in town."

"Good idea!" someone from the crowd shouted. "That's a weird name!"

"Oh, but she doesn't live here." Laura was thinking

fast. "She lives in some little town a few miles from here."

"Which one?" Alexis demanded.

Laura shrugged. "I have no idea." She smiled. "Sorry."

Alexis glared at Laura. Then she glanced helplessly around. "Don't you all think it's pretty convenient that everything I suggest won't work?" she asked, loudly enough for everyone in the crowd to hear. "There doesn't seem to be any way that Laura can possibly prove her maid story."

"Except if you come to my apartment tomorrow morning," Laura said with a small, triumphant smile.

Once again she glanced around to see if anyone would take her up on her offer. There were still no takers. She breathed a silent sigh of relief.

Alexis took a step backward, then whirled around and marched away down the hall. A large group of kids followed her, among them The Fabulous Five, Laura noticed. She watched them go. She was pretty sure she had won the battle.

Then she looked at the few kids still hanging around. Thank goodness Shane was gone—and she didn't think he had followed Alexis. Some kids were starting to leave now, but others were glancing sideways at her. *They still didn't believe her!*

Maybe she hadn't won the battle after all.

Laura turned to Tammy, Funny, and Melissa. "I guess I settled that," she declared, watching her friends' faces carefully.

Tammy stared at Laura as if she were searching for the truth in Laura's face. Funny and Melissa looked at the floor.

"What's the matter with you guys?" Laura demanded.

Funny finally looked up at Laura. "Laura," she said evenly, "*we* haven't even seen your maid—and we're your best friends."

"So you have to see my maid before you believe me?" Laura huffed. "Some friends!"

Tammy gasped. "But we *are* your friends!"

"Real friends stand by each other," Laura said. "They don't doubt each other's honesty."

"I don't doubt you," Tammy insisted. "Can't you believe that?"

Laura turned away.

"What can I do to prove I'm your friend?" Tammy asked.

Laura thought she could detect desperation in Tammy's voice. She was glad that *someone* felt desperate about being her friend.

"We're your friends, too," Funny said softly. "But it would be fun to see Chantal sometime."

"Because you really want to meet her?" asked Laura, "or so that you can know I'm not lying?"

There was a long pause.

"I'd like to meet her," Funny said, staring Laura right in the eyes.

"Did you notice that The Fabulous Five left with Alexis?" asked Laura abruptly, changing the subject.

"Yeah," the girls mumbled.

"They're on Alexis's side, you know," Laura warned. "That could mean big trouble for The Fantastic Four-some if they talk the rest of the kids into siding with her. Our group could be history."

"That's true," agreed Melissa.

"We've got to stick together," Tammy added. "Through thick and thin."

"We *will* stick together," said Laura, "if you help me and stick up for me."

"Don't worry," Tammy assured her. "We won't let you down again."

"Can I depend on you two?" Laura asked Funny and Melissa.

"You can depend on me," Melissa answered.

"How about you, Funny?"

Funny nodded, not looking at Laura. "I'm with you," she said softly.

Laura felt a little better, but not a lot. Somehow she wasn't completely convinced.

CHAPTER

9

"*Gone With the Wind* is my all-time favorite movie," said Tammy, plopping onto the floor in front of the television set. "Don't you think Vivien Leigh is *gorgeous?*"

Laura set a huge bowl of popcorn down in front of Funny and Melissa. "I like Clark Gable, myself."

"Well, I wish you'd gotten *Bill and Ted's Excellent Adventure*," said Funny. "It's the most hilarious movie I've ever seen."

"Can't you ever be serious?" Melissa grumbled.

Funny gave her a pained look.

"All the copies were checked out, anyway," said Laura before Funny could fire back an angry response. She had invited the girls to come over on Friday evening to watch the rented movie. She needed the time alone with them to work on their friendship—and their loyalty. The last thing she needed was Funny and Melissa squabbling among themselves.

She had scrubbed the apartment last night and baked more cookies. She'd dug into her wallet and bought three six-packs of soda, lots of popcorn, and real butter to drizzle over the hot popcorn. This time she made sure to check her bureau mirror for any notes from her father as soon as she got home. There weren't any.

So far everything seemed to be going pretty well. Funny and Melissa were a little quiet, but they were smiling. Laura thought that things might just be getting back to normal.

Tonight her friends didn't mention the maid or how great the apartment looked. Laura had gone to a lot of trouble, but she didn't mind when no one gushed over how clean the place was or how good the cookies tasted. She had more important things on her mind.

The movie started, and Scarlett O'Hara was surrounded by handsome Southern gentlemen, talking and flirting with her on the veranda of her sprawling plantation home.

Tammy sighed. "Imagine being surrounded by good-looking, rich guys who all want you! Can you think of anything more wonderful?"

Laura grinned. "It's fun, all right."

Melissa shot her a mean look. "Yeah, right, McCall. Tell us all about it."

Laura was startled. What was wrong? In her mind she played back what she'd just said.

I get it, she thought. Melissa must be jealous.

Ordinarily, Melissa's sarcastic remark would have prompted her to make a nasty retort. But she couldn't afford to do that right now. She had to get The Fantastic Foursome on her side. Her future at Wakeman was riding on the next few days.

"I mean," Laura said, trying to smooth things over, "I mean, it must be fun to have that much attention from cute guys."

No one said anything.

Hmph, Laura thought. I could have told them about the time at the swimming pool when I was visiting my cousin in Minneapolis. Within twenty minutes we were surrounded by six cute boys who were all flirting with us. One of them was in high school!

But they wouldn't appreciate the story tonight, she decided. Maybe another time.

She heard a key in the lock, and in walked her father and Trudy.

"Hi, everyone!" Mr. McCall said.

"Hi, Daddy," said Laura.

"Hi, Mr. McCall," the other three girls chorused.

"Trudy," Laura said, "these are my friends, Funny, Melissa, and Tammy. Guys, this is Trudy Dwyer."

The three girls and Trudy exchanged hellos.

Trudy looked great again. She was wearing a short black skirt, black textured hose and a yellow tank top with a blouse over that.

"Hey, Trudy," said Laura. "I like your outfit."

Trudy looked pleased. "Thanks, Laura. I like yours—this time."

"Dad, isn't Trudy's skirt cute?" Laura asked.

"Certainly is," her dad said.

"Good, I'm glad you like it." Laura grinned. "Because it's exactly like my black one—the one you made me change last week."

Mr. McCall rolled his eyes. "I should have guessed."

Trudy laughed and playfully socked him in the arm. "She's too smart for you, Walker," she said.

Laura smiled triumphantly and turned back to the movie.

"Thanks for letting us come over tonight," Tammy said to Laura's father. "I just love this movie."

"Sure thing," Mr. McCall replied. "You girls are welcome any time."

Tammy sighed. "If only my parents would say things like that." She stared off into the distance. "I guess when you have a maid, you aren't so uptight about having guests."

Laura almost rocketed out of her chair. *Did Tammy say what I thought she said?*

"If you have a what?" asked Mr. McCall.

"A mai—"

"I know!" Laura interrupted frantically. "Let's play cards while we watch the movie!"

She jumped up and ran to the small desk next to the window. Opening the drawer, she grabbed the cards, then slammed the drawer shut again and ran back to where the girls were sitting.

"How about hearts?" Laura asked in a loud voice. "Know how to play that? Or rummy? How about gin rummy?" She looked around the room wildly.

Tammy, Melissa, Funny, her father, and Trudy were all staring at her, their mouths open.

Trudy leaned toward Laura's father and spoke in a low voice, but Laura heard what she said. "Is she always this hyper?"

Laura forced a laugh. "Oh, it just seemed to be time for a game. Anybody want to play?"

"I do!" Tammy spoke up. She still sounded desperate to please Laura.

"How about you guys?" she asked Funny and Melissa.

"No thanks," Funny answered. "I want to concentrate on the movie."

"Me, too," said Melissa.

Laura pretended not to care. At least she had Tammy's attention. Now Tammy wouldn't make any more dumb remarks to her father about having a maid and blow everything. She shrugged. "Suits me fine."

"We just came home to get the theater tickets," her father explained. "I forgot them."

"Okay," said Laura. "See you later."

Laura and Tammy spent most of the rest of the evening playing cards while Funny and Melissa watched the movie.

This isn't going the way I'd planned, Laura said to herself. I wanted the four of us to have fun together, the way we used to, so everyone would remember how much our friendship means. If only Tammy hadn't made that stupid comment to Dad about the maid.

The movie was almost over, and Laura picked up the cards and put them away.

"This was really fun, Laura." Tammy sounded enthusiastic. "Thanks for inviting us."

"Sure," said Laura.

She noticed that Melissa and Funny didn't add their thanks.

When the movie was over, Tammy called her parents to pick her up. "Want a ride home?" she asked Melissa and Funny.

"No, thanks," Funny said, and shot Melissa a warning look.

What's this all about? Laura wondered. They always go home together.

In twenty minutes Tammy's father arrived. Tammy threw on her coat. "Sure we can't drop you guys off?"

"No, thanks," Funny repeated.

"Okay," said Tammy. She turned to go, then turned back. "Hey, tomorrow's Saturday. Are you going to the mall?"

"I'm going to sleep in," Laura told her. "But I'll probably get there by noon."

"Great," said Tammy. "See you tomorrow."

She disappeared out the door.

Laura looked questioningly at Funny and Melissa, who were standing awkwardly in the middle of the living room.

"Thanks for the movie," Funny said.

"Sure," replied Laura.

"Uh, can we talk to you?" asked Funny.

Laura's stomach tightened. "What about?"

"About Tammy," Melissa answered.

Laura immediately relaxed. For an instant she had been afraid they would bring up the maid story.

"Sure," she said. "What about Tammy?"

Funny shifted her weight over to one foot and glanced at Melissa.

"What's the matter?" Laura insisted.

"Well," Melissa began, "Tammy has started another rumor."

Alarms went off inside Laura. "What rumor?" she demanded.

"About Alexis," said Funny.

Laura frowned. "What's she saying now?"

"Tammy is telling everyone that she glanced into

your room that day at the party—" Funny began, and paused.

"She's telling everybody that she saw Alexis's reflection in the mirror over your bureau," Melissa finished for her.

"Go on," Laura pressed.

"Well, Tammy is saying that she wasn't sure what Alexis was up to," Funny said, "so she signaled *you* to check it out."

"And that was when you caught Alexis going through your things," Melissa put in.

There was a moment of silence.

"And, of course, you know that's not true," Funny concluded in a little voice. "Tammy was out in the living room the whole time. She couldn't possibly have seen down the hall and into your room."

"She just made up the story," Melissa said.

Laura gulped. "But why?"

Melissa looked Laura straight in the eyes. "Because she really likes you, Laura. She would do almost anything for you. Even lie."

There was another awkward silence.

"Well, I still don't see why Tammy would do that," said Laura.

"Don't you get it?" Funny asked in astonishment. "People are more likely to believe your story if it's two people against one. Tammy did it so that everyone would believe that Alexis is lying."

Laura's stomach felt tied in knots. It was obvious that Funny and Melissa still didn't believe her.

"Maybe you'll give some thought to Alexis and this whole situation over the weekend," Funny suggested hopefully.

Laura's eyes narrowed. "And why would I want to waste a perfectly good weekend thinking about Alexis? She accused me in public of lying!"

"Alexis has a very good reputation," Funny said gently. "Everybody likes her."

"Just what are you trying to say?" asked Laura, her voice rising in anger.

"Just that—" Funny stammered a little, "just that I like her, too."

"And you believe her and not me?" Laura demanded, her teeth clenched tightly and her eyes blazing.

"I didn't say that," Funny replied. "I just like her."

"So do I," Melissa offered.

"More than you like The Fantastic Foursome?" asked Laura. "If The Fantastic Foursome means *anything* to you, you'd better be careful! You'd better choose sides very carefully, do you hear me?"

Funny gazed at Laura calmly. "I don't think I want to choose sides. I think I'd like to have lots of friends." Turning to Melissa, she added, "I think we'd better go now."

"Good idea," said Melissa.

Laura's mouth dropped open. *Never* had the other girls in The Fantastic Foursome doubted her, *never* had any of them walked away from her when she was angry. *And Funny and Melissa looked so calm! They were practically breaking up The Fantastic Foursome, and they didn't even look upset!*

"We'll be at the mall tomorrow," Funny told her. "If you feel like coming, we'll see you there."

The two girls disappeared through the door. Laura stood stiffly in the middle of the living room and listened to their footsteps disappear down the hall.

She felt completely and utterly alone.

CHAPTER

10

The mall was crowded with Saturday shoppers by the time Laura arrived the next morning. She hadn't slept well during the night, but the adrenaline rushing through her kept her alert as she thought about meeting The Fantastic Foursome.

Tammy, Funny, and Melissa. What was happening with them? Would they get through this and remain friends? Laura had never felt so out of control. Any moment her group might break up.

Tammy at least was loyal. She would do anything for Laura. And wasn't that the way friendship should be? Maybe only Tammy would remain her friend. Was it possible to have a group of only two? Well, it wouldn't have to be just two. Practically every girl in seventh grade was dying to get into The Fantastic Foursome. *Her* clique! After all, Laura McCall was *somebody* at Wakeman.

But the thought of a new clique without Funny and Melissa was awful. Would two of her very best friends become her enemies? Would they talk about her behind her back, and start hanging around with The Fabulous Five? Funny was already good friends with Jana Morgan.

That was too much even to think about. Laura willed herself to think about other things.

Laura headed for Taco Plenty, the usual meeting spot for The Fantastic Foursome. She spotted Melissa, Funny, and Tammy already sitting together in their favorite spot along the edge of the eating area. Funny always said it was a perfect place to see "the action." What she meant was it was a perfect place to watch the boys go by. Her friends were leaning over their sodas and talking. They didn't see her coming.

I'm going to be really up, Laura decided. Funny and Melissa will think that what they said last night didn't faze me a bit!

"Hi, everybody," she called, as she approached the girls' table. She planted a friendly smile on her face.

"Hi," Tammy said brightly. "Sit down."

Laura sat down, still careful to keep the smile firmly in place, and glanced at Funny and Melissa. They were watching her carefully, probably curious about how she would act after the scene last night.

"Any kids around?" she asked, trying to sound casual.

"Shane was over by the mall entrance when we came in," reported Funny with her usual giggle. "We've been keeping an eye on him for you."

Instinctively Laura spun around and looked over her shoulder. "I didn't see him," she said. "Maybe he'll come by here in a few minutes."

"Beth Barry and Jana Morgan and Melanie Edwards are sitting over there." Melissa nodded across the courtyard.

"Great," Laura said sarcastically. "Who else?"

"Some eighth-graders are getting burritos," replied Melissa. "More kids should get here pretty soon."

"Oh, there's Sara Sawyer," said Funny, looking up from her soda. "She's with Lisa Snow."

Laura's stomach flipped over. Sara and Lisa were Alexis's best friends. That meant Alexis would probably show up, too.

Laura wanted to avoid Sara and Lisa.

"Want to do some shopping at Juniors' Jungle?" she asked.

"Sure," Tammy piped up.

"Yeah, I'll come, too," said Funny. "I heard there's a sale on jeans."

"What're we waiting for?" asked Melissa.

The girls got up and trooped down the mall corridor.

"Hi, Laura. Hi, everybody!"

The voice belonged to Shane Arrington. He was leaning up against a support pillar in the corridor, with a big grin on his face. Laura felt her heart flutter. He was *so* cute. She would die if he turned against her. So what if he was dating Melanie Edwards? That couldn't last forever.

"Hi, Shane," called Laura. Then a new thought occurred to her. He must believe me instead of Alexis. Otherwise he wouldn't be so friendly.

The girls clustered around him.

"So what's goin' on?" He was asking everyone, but he was looking at Laura.

Her heart fluttered faster. "Not too much," she replied.

"Hey, what's all this stuff about Alexis?" he asked. "I can't believe she'd steal anything, but I guess you never know."

A sudden burst of giggles from Funny jolted Laura to attention. She threw a warning look at Funny, who shrank back in embarrassment. Funny and her stupid giggling, Laura thought angrily, and her rotten sense of timing. Laura forced a smile as she turned back to Shane. "What did you say?" she asked sweetly.

"I was talking about Alexis," Shane said, "and how

hard it is to imagine her stealing, but I guess you never know about anybody."

Laura shrugged. "I guess not," she said. Feeling Funny's and Melissa's eyes boring into her, she decided to change the subject. "How's Igor, Shane?"

Igor was Shane's pet iguana. If you asked Shane about Igor, you instantly became his friend.

Shane grinned. "Terrific, how else? He made the whole family pancakes for breakfast this morning. What a cook! He didn't even use a cookbook."

The girls giggled, and Laura was relieved to see that Funny and Melissa seemed to have forgotten Alexis.

"Igor gets smarter every day," remarked Funny. "Last week you said he repaired your mom's washing machine."

"Yup," said Shane. A wide smile broke across his face. "He got straight A's in technical school."

Funny giggled. "I can just see him picking up his diploma at graduation."

"Hey, he looked totally handsome in his cap and flowing red gown." Shane's tone was perfectly serious.

"Red?" asked Melissa.

"The technical school's colors," Shane explained. "Red and white."

Laura laughed, feeling the release of tension in her group.

"We're on our way to Juniors' Jungle," Funny told him. "Want to come along?"

Shane rolled his eyes. "Yeah, right, and sit around while you girls try on clothes." He grinned. "Not my idea of a great time."

The girls said good-bye and started to move away.

"Oh, and Laura—" he called after them.

Laura turned around.

"Hang in there," Shane said, giving her a thumbs-up sign.

Laura felt a rush of relief. Shane was on her side. "Thanks," she said.

Melissa snorted and shook her head.

"What's the matter?" Tammy asked Melissa, loud enough for Laura to hear.

"Never mind," Melissa mumbled. "Just never mind."

Laura glanced at Melissa and felt the worry creep into the pit of her stomach again. She was losing Melissa and Funny, even though she seemed to be gaining the confidence of some of the other kids.

Laura felt a hand on her arm. "There's Alexis," Tammy whispered.

Alexis was standing with Sara Sawyer and Lisa Snow. Laura blinked and then frowned. Alexis looked awful! She had dark circles under her eyes, her hair was stringy, her shoulders were stooped, and she looked exhausted.

"I wonder what's the matter with her," said Tammy.

"Maybe she's feeling as if no one likes her anymore," Funny responded, looking daggers at Laura.

"That's ridiculous," snapped Laura. "She's one of the most popular girls in school."

"Maybe she used to be," Melissa replied, looking directly at Tammy. "Before *rumors* about her being a thief started to fly around."

Laura was silent. But inside her head, questions screamed out to be answered. *What am I going to do? How can I possibly get out of this mess?*

"I don't want to see Alexis," said Funny. "Let's get out of here."

"Good idea," agreed Melissa.

"Let's look in here," Tammy suggested, heading into a store.

"It's for *guys*!" Laura said, pointing to the display in the window.

But it was too late to stop her friends. Funny, Melissa, and Tammy had already gone into the store and were disappearing behind racks of men's suits.

"Laura," came a voice from behind her.

Laura whirled around to see Alexis, Lisa, and Sara.

"Hi." Laura felt her heart suddenly beating wildly.

"Laura, I need to talk to you," said Alexis.

Laura knew she was trapped. "Okay."

Alexis motioned to Lisa and Sara to leave them

alone. Then she led Laura to a bench in the middle of the mall.

Alexis turned around to face Laura, and Laura could see the defeat in her eyes.

"Well, I give up, Laura," Alexis said. Her voice was lifeless.

"What?" Laura asked incredulously.

"Just what I said. I give up."

"I don't know what you mean," Laura replied.

"You set out to get me," said Alexis. "You told everyone I'm a thief just to cover up your own lies, and now you and Tammy have everybody believing you."

Laura could feel the heat climbing up her neck. She didn't speak.

"I just wanted you to know that I'm not going to fight you anymore," Alexis continued. "You win."

"I win?" Laura whispered.

"That's right. You win. I won't protest anymore. You can say whatever you want and get Tammy to back you up. I'm tired of fighting you."

Laura opened her mouth, but nothing came out. She closed it again.

"I'm tired of trying to prove myself to kids at school. My real friends know the truth—that I'm innocent—but I can't prove to everybody else that you made up that story. And guess what? I don't even want to try anymore. You win. Congratulations."

There was no sarcasm in Alexis's voice. Only defeat. And sadness.

Alexis turned and walked away toward the mall's exit.

Laura stood there for a long time, watching as Alexis's form got smaller and smaller.

She felt a strange emptiness inside.

CHAPTER

11

"So what did Alexis want?" Tammy asked over the telephone. "You left the mall so fast, we didn't get a chance to ask you."

"Yeah, um well—"

"We saw Alexis come up and say she wanted to talk to you," Tammy interrupted.

"Right," Laura confirmed, sinking onto her bed. A phone conversation with Tammy Lucero was the last thing in the world she wanted right now. "She . . . she just wanted to talk."

"What did she say?" Tammy persisted.

"Well, she—I guess she isn't going to fight anymore," Laura said.

"Good!" exclaimed Tammy. "Now maybe people will believe you."

"Believe me?" Laura echoed, her mind still whirling from Alexis's surprise announcement at the mall and the miserable look on her face when she made it.

"About your maid," Tammy said. "Alexis made it sound as if you were the one who was lying."

"Oh. Yeah, I know," Laura murmured, but somehow Tammy's words didn't make her feel any better.

"Hey, how come you disappeared so fast from the mall?" asked Tammy. "Funny, Melissa, and I looked all over for you."

"Uh, I just didn't feel well," Laura mumbled. "I'm sorry I didn't say good-bye."

"Oh, well—that's okay. We just wondered where you'd gone. We thought maybe Alexis had said something that made you want to leave."

"Oh, no," Laura protested. "I . . . I got a stomachache."

"Gosh, that's too bad. Feeling better?"

"Yeah," answered Laura.

"Great," Tammy said. "Well . . . see you at school on Monday."

"Right." Laura hung up the phone and lay back on her bed.

Why does life have to be so complicated? she wondered. She thought back to the day she had invented the story about having a maid. It seemed like a million years ago. What had The Fantastic Foursome been talking about, anyway?

Oh, yes, she remembered. Melissa had made some comment about what she was wearing. Her clothes looked old and wrinkled, or something like that. So Laura had started that harmless little lie. And that one teensy lie had snowballed and snowballed until it turned into a total disaster. If only Melissa hadn't made that nasty remark about her shirt.

That's right, Laura thought, sitting up again. Melissa had started the whole thing. If she hadn't been so critical of Laura, this mess would never have happened. Laura frowned as she thought about Melissa. If The Fantastic Foursome split up, maybe it wouldn't be so bad not to have Melissa-the-Perfect around always criticizing!

"But Melissa didn't start the lie," whispered a little voice in her mind. "*You* did."

Laura sighed. She felt sad, tired, and fed up with people. She had done all she could to keep everything under control. Melissa's pickiness and Tammy's big mouth were a lot to put up with.

Laura thought about Alexis. Poor Alexis. She had looked so awful at the mall. So disappointed in everything. And so hurt.

A rush of guilt washed over Laura. She really liked Alexis. It made her feel terrible to think she had hurt her.

Well, Laura corrected herself indignantly, I really wasn't the one who hurt Alexis. It was Tammy who spread the rumors about her. If Tammy had minded her own business and kept her mouth shut the way I told her to, Alexis wouldn't be so hurt, The Fantastic Foursome wouldn't be about to break up, and I wouldn't be so miserable.

"But Tammy wasn't the one who lied," whispered the little voice.

I can't blame it on anyone but myself, she thought.

Laura rolled over on her stomach. She had to figure out a way to get out of this horrible mess. But most important, she knew she had to make things right again.

It had all started with the maid. That stupid, rotten maid—

An idea flashed in Laura's mind. She stretched out on the bed and let her mind play with the thought and develop it.

That's it! she thought excitedly when she had it worked out just right. The maid had started this whole thing. And now the maid would get her out of it!

All the kids at school greeted Laura with friendly smiles and waves on Monday morning. Tammy must have spread the word about Alexis, she realized. They're all on my side now.

Laura thought about letting go of the whole incident and not going through her with plan. It was tempting. Even the best plans could backfire, and if hers backfired, everyone would know she had lied.

Laura went into the empty bathroom before lunch and into one of the stalls. A minute later she heard the bathroom door open and feet shuffle in.

"It's so hard to believe," a voice said. Laura recognized it as Beth Barry's.

"I know," replied her friend Jana Morgan. "Alexis has always been such a great person. How could she possibly have done something awful like *steal*?"

Laura peeked at the girls through the crack in the door. Jana and Beth were brushing their hair in front of the mirror.

"I can't believe it, either," Beth said. "But when you've got the word of two people—even when those two people happen to be Laura McCall and Tammy Lucero—against one person, you have to wonder a little."

Laura gritted her teeth at the mention of her name.

"I always thought Alexis was almost perfect," Jana commented. "She gets good grades, she's nice to people, she has lots of friends—"

"Not so many now," Beth interrupted. "I heard that

Sally and Jennifer had planned to invite her to their party, but now they've decided not to. They say they're not going to hang around with her until it's proven one way or the other if she's a thief."

"They're afraid Alexis might steal from them?" asked Jana.

"Right," said Beth.

"Wow," exclaimed Jana. "I thought in this country we're supposed to be innocent until proven guilty."

"But have you seen Alexis today?" asked Beth. "She looks like something the cat dragged in! She's acting weird, too, keeping to herself, walking along the hall as close to the lockers as she can get."

"I don't know what to think," said Jana. "I'm going to be nice to her, but I'm going to be careful, too. It's just so sad."

The girls filed out of the bathroom.

As soon as they were gone, Laura opened the stall door and moved to the mirror. She took out some blush from her backpack and brushed it on, all the while thinking about Alexis.

If Jana and Beth were questioning Alexis's honesty, then *everybody* must be wondering about her.

Laura looked at herself in the mirror. She suddenly didn't like what she saw. Oh, sure, she was still good-looking. It wasn't that. She just felt different about herself the last few days.

She thought about the lie for the millionth time.

Laura hadn't planned to hurt anybody. But she had ended up lying about Alexis to protect herself. She had told the lie only to her friends, true, but Tammy had spread it. And now she felt like the world's biggest jerk. She felt as if she had a rock in her stomach. She was sick of feeling this way, sick of the whole thing.

She had to put her plan into action—right now. She stuffed the blush into her backpack and hurried out of the bathroom.

CHAPTER

12

Laura slipped into her place at the lunch table.

"Hi, Laura," Tammy said brightly.

Funny and Melissa barely acknowledged her. They nodded slightly and went back to their conversation. Laura's stomach twisted painfully. She hoped that her plan would not only save Alexis's reputation, but also get Laura herself back in the good graces of her friends. She knew now that it wasn't just their loyalty she wanted, it was their genuine friendship.

"Hi, everyone," Laura said. She cleared her throat. "Could I interrupt you guys for a minute?"

Melissa rolled her eyes, but she and Funny stopped talking.

"I'm calling a meeting after school today," Laura announced.

"Of The Fantastic Foursome?" Tammy asked.

"Yes, but I'm asking Alexis, Lisa, Sara, and Marcie to come, too," said Laura.

Funny frowned. "Are you sure you want to do that?"

"Don't you think there's been enough trouble already?" asked Melissa. "I don't think I can stomach any more bad scenes for a while."

"There won't be any bad scenes," Laura insisted. "I just want to talk to everybody. I promise you the results will be good."

"And peaceful?" asked Funny.

"And peaceful," Laura assured her.

Funny and Melissa exchanged glances.

"No offense, Laura," Funny said, "but you're not exactly known for promoting peace."

Laura bit her tongue. She didn't want to blow her plan by getting mad and causing an uproar.

"You'll have to trust me." Laura's jaws clenched tightly.

"I'll be there!" Tammy said.

"Good. Come to our spot next to the building right after the final bell." She looked at Funny and Melissa. "Will you two be there?"

They both nodded.

"Good," Laura said, standing up. "See you there."

"Aren't you going to eat?" asked Tammy.

"I'm not hungry," Laura replied. "And I have some things to do. See you after school."

Laura moved away from the table and glanced around the cafeteria until she spotted Alexis sitting with The Fabulous Five. Swallowing hard, she marched to their table.

It was Alexis who first saw Laura coming. She dropped her sandwich, and her face turned ashen. The others, who had been chatting together, stopped talking and watched Laura approach.

This was one time Laura wasn't happy about being in the spotlight.

"Alexis," Laura began, "I'd like to talk to you after school. My friends will be there, and you should bring yours, too." She nodded toward the girls at the table.

Melanie leaned over to Katie and whispered loudly enough for everyone to hear. "Do you think this means war?"

"No, Melanie," said Laura, "this is not war. I just have something to say, and I want everybody to be there to hear it."

Alexis seemed to shrink into her seat. She looked afraid.

"Meet me beside the school after the final bell," Laura instructed. "Please. Will you be there?"

There was a pause while everyone waited for Alexis to respond. "Okay," she answered in a small voice.

"And we'll be with her," Katie declared firmly.

"Good," said Laura. "See you then."

She turned and left the lunchroom. She really wasn't hungry. She just wanted to get this over with.

The afternoon crawled by. Finally the last bell sounded. Laura rushed to her locker and got what she needed to take home tonight. Then she headed for The Fantastic Foursome's spot beside the school.

Tammy was the first to arrive. "Hi," she said. "This is really exciting, Laura, and mysterious! I can't wait to find out what's going on."

"You'll find out in a few minutes," Laura told her, "after everyone gets here."

She hoped that would be right away, but for the next five minutes no one showed up.

What's going on? she wondered. Doesn't anyone care what I have to say?

Tammy stood next to her, chattering away, but Laura barely heard a word of it. She was worried. Why was everyone taking so long?

Finally she saw Funny and Melissa walking toward her. They both looked doubtful, and Laura knew they were a little afraid of what might happen.

Then Laura saw Alexis. She was surrounded by Marcie, Sara, and Lisa. The three friends were obviously giving Alexis encouragement to face Laura one more time.

And just behind Alexis and her friends were The Fabulous Five, without Christie Winchell. Laura was glad they had come, too. Maybe they would see her differently after this afternoon's meeting.

"Hi, everyone." Laura spoke softly when they were all there.

No one replied, but everyone stared at her. Hard.

"So what's up?" Beth Barry said finally. It wasn't just a question; it was a demand to know what Laura had up her sleeve.

"I have something to say to Alexis and to all of you," she began shakily.

"Okay," said Lisa with a shrug. "So say it."

Laura could feel hostility in the air, but she forced herself to stay calm.

"Okay, what I want to say is this: You can't meet my maid—"

"Haven't we heard this before?" demanded Alexis, taking a step forward. "We can't meet your maid because she only comes while—"

"—we're at school!" the others chorused. There were giggles through the group.

"No!" said Laura, her voice starting to rise with anger. *Get hold of yourself,* she reminded herself silently. *Say what you planned to say, and don't let them get to you.* "No!" she repeated, this time in a more controlled voice. "You can't meet my maid because we don't have a maid anymore."

Alexis let out a shriek. "That's very convenient!" she shouted. "You don't have a maid anymore."

Katie Shannon took a step forward. "Yeah. You expect us to believe you had a maid in the first place—"

"Just let me finish!" Laura pleaded desperately. "Let me say what I have to say."

"Go ahead," Alexis said, her eyes still flashing with anger and frustration.

"I was wrong about one thing," Laura continued. "Chantal wasn't such a great person after all."

"I thought you all *loved* each other," remarked Beth sarcastically.

"Well, we misjudged her, I guess," Laura said. "She wasn't the loyal employee we thought she was." Laura paused, studying their faces for some clue about what they were thinking. Their faces revealed nothing, except that they were listening intently. "Dad fired her yesterday."

The girls gasped. "*Fired* her?" Lisa exclaimed. "But why? What did she do?"

"My dad caught her stealing," said Laura.

A murmur ran through her listeners.

"And when Dad confronted Chantal," Laura went on, "she admitted it." Laura glanced at the faces around her. "When he demanded the stolen things back, she brought out some other stuff she'd taken from the apartment, too."

Laura reached into her shirt pocket and pulled out a Wakeman charm bracelet. She held it up.

"This is one of the things she had stolen," Laura told the crowd. "My charm bracelet."

"But you said—" Alexis started.

Laura nodded and pulled a second bracelet out of the pocket of her jeans. "Yeah, and I feel pretty crummy. See, I thought yours belonged to me because of the scratch on the tepee. But *both* of these bracelets are scratched—in the same place."

The girls moved in close to see the scratch that Laura had carefully made this morning before she'd left for school. She had also removed her cheerleading charm so that the two bracelets looked identical.

"Alexis," Laura said, "I'm sorry I suspected you. But can't you see now how I made the mistake?"

Alexis looked at the scratch on the bracelet and then at Laura. "But I never would have stolen anything from you, Laura," she insisted.

"Well, I know that *now*," Laura said quietly. "But I . . . well, I didn't know it then. I'm sorry." She glanced at Tammy. "And I guess Tammy just misunderstood the situation in my bedroom, too."

"Oh, yes, and I'm so sorry, Alexis!" Tammy sputtered, grateful to Laura for explaining her part in the episode.

"It was probably the maid who left the drawer open

on the bureau," Laura said. "And after I'd seen you standing in my room—well, naturally I suspected you, Alexis. But I was wrong, and I'm sorry."

The girls all seemed to relax a little. They stepped back and looked at each other, obviously grateful to have this whole thing cleared up. Some of them started to move away.

Laura took Alexis's arm and drew her away from the others. "Remember when I came into my bedroom and found you?" said Laura. "And I told you it was the maid's day off?"

Alexis nodded.

"Well," Laura went on, "what I said was true. Chantal *hadn't* been at the apartment that morning, but she'd cleaned and made our snacks the night before."

"Okay," Alexis said. "I guess you were telling me the truth."

Laura smiled in relief. She knew she was lying again, but she was glad that one last lie would put the whole mess to rest. And it would be the *last lie*—that was for certain. Lies just weren't worth it. Her stomach began to unknot for the first time in days.

"I'm sorry I believed the worst of you," Laura finished.

Alexis hesitated for a moment. "I liked it a whole lot better when we were friends," she finally admitted.

Laura smiled. "Me, too."

"Think we can forget all this?" Alexis asked softly.

"Can you?" said Laura.

Alexis paused and ran a hand through her hair thoughtfully. "Yes, I guess so."

Laura beamed. "I was really hoping you would say that!"

Alexis smiled and put out her hand. "Friends?"

"Friends," said Laura, shaking Alexis's hand.

After Alexis and her friends had gone, Melissa heaved a sigh of relief and said, "Boy, am I ever glad that's over."

"See, I *told* you that you'd like this meeting," Laura teased.

"Yeah," said Funny with a tinkling little laugh. "It had a happy ending after all."

"And you've got your giggle back," commented Laura.

Laura felt better as she watched Alexis walk away with her head up, her shoulders squared, and a smile on her face. She felt better about her own friends, too. They liked her again. She knew that in their own way, they had been her friends all along. I'll never do anything that could damage our friendship again, she promised herself.

For an instant she remembered how she had covered up her own mistake—spilling blush on her blouse—by blaming it on someone else. I'll definitely never lie again, because one lie leads to another and another, and pretty soon the whole world's a disaster area. But even my friends make mistakes, she thought. They're not perfect, but I like them, anyway. Maybe they can get used to me the way I *really* am, too.

The four friends walked along in silence for a few moments. Then Funny stopped abruptly and grinned at Laura.

"You know," she said, "I always thought I'd love to have a maid at our house." She giggled. "But after all the trouble a maid caused at *your* house, I'm not so sure!"

Laura looked at Funny and smiled. *Amen to that!* Laura agreed silently. *Amen to that!*

Laura knew something was up as soon as she walked into the apartment. Her dad and Trudy were in the kitchen. Trudy was getting down some glasses from the cupboard, and her dad was holding a bottle of something—was it champagne?

Laura froze. Her dad and Trudy were obviously going to toast something. They had been seeing a lot of each other lately. Could it be—the thought would barely form in her mind—*marriage plans*? That would be a hundred times more traumatic than that dumb lie about the maid!

They looked up as she entered and smiled at her.

"Laura," her father said. "I have a surprise for you."

"I'm not sure I want to hear this," Laura replied, swallowing hard.

"Of course you do. Come here. I'll pour you a glass of soda so you can join our toast. We have some wonderful news that includes you."

Laura stood stiffly while her father poured the soft drink. She looked at Trudy, who grinned and nodded and looked very happy.

"Let's toast this very special day," Mr. McCall said, holding up his glass of champagne. "I've been waiting for this to happen for a very long time."

"Don't I have any say in it?" Laura blurted out.

Her father looked startled. "You don't even know what I'm going to say." He stared hard at his daughter and then glanced over at Trudy. "Laura, baby, I don't think you understand. I got the promotion!"

A smile began to creep across Laura's face. "Ohhhh, the promotion!" she cried.

Her father laughed and hugged her. "What in the world did you *think* I meant?"

Laura glanced at Trudy, who winked at her knowingly.

"I think," said Trudy, "that Laura was afraid something more serious and long-lasting was being celebrated here."

Mr. McCall's face tinted pink.

Laura laughed. "Daddy, you're blushing."

"Well, wait till you hear *this*," her father said, and

Laura knew he was changing the subject as quickly as he could. "I know I've been pretty demanding lately."

"Yes, you have," Laura agreed, smiling. "So what else is new?"

"What a smart-alecky kid," said her father in mock anger, shaking his head. "Anyway, I know that your life is very busy, and this is the time you should be having fun."

"I won't argue with that!" replied Laura.

"Well, I think I've been a *little* bit unreasonable about the housework. Soooo, here's the news. Are you ready?"

Laura nodded.

"I've decided that you deserve a break, so . . . I've hired a maid!" her father announced proudly.

"A mai—" Laura said faintly. Her eyes got big. "A MAID?"

Then she exploded with laughter. She laughed and laughed until tears rolled down her cheeks and plopped on the kitchen table.

Mr. McCall and Trudy stared at each other with bewildered expressions on their faces. Which made Laura laugh all the harder.

Here's a preview of The Fabulous Five #27, *The Scapegoat*, coming to your bookstore soon.

*C*hristie Winchell rubbed her eyes in disbelief at the clock on her dresser. It was almost eleven o'clock. Where had the time gone? She had started studying right after supper and had just finished in time to go to bed.

School was certainly a lot harder in London. Especially Miss Finney's science class. It seemed as if Christie couldn't get anything right in science, no matter how hard she tried. Every time she thought she had her homework done perfectly, Miss Finney found tons of things wrong with it. It was almost as if she had something against Christie.

Christie closed her science book and shoved it away, stretching and yawning. Things were different in a lot of ways at St. Margaret's. For one thing her friends in The Fabulous Five weren't there. Although she was starting to make friends with Phoebe, Nicki, and Eleanore, it still wasn't quite the same.

And then there was Chase Collins. She missed him a lot. Christie smiled. She had to admit, it was nice that he wrote so often. She really hadn't expected him to live up to the things that he said, especially since her family might never move back to the United States.

She got up and took off her school uniform and slipped into her robe. Next she took the four bears her friends had given her when she left America, along with her tennis bear, and lined them up on the chair next to the bed.

"You guys wait here," she ordered as she went to the bathroom to wash her face.

"Maybe if I talk to Miss Finney and tell her how much I like science, she won't be so tough on me all the time," Christie said to the soapy face in the mirror. She shook her head. No, she thought stubbornly. I'll just prove it to her by working extra hard.

But Christie has never had to deal with someone in authority who doesn't like her. Will she be able to prove herself to Miss Finney? Find out in The Fabulous Five #27: *The Scapegoat*.

Do you and your friends know the answers to these trivia questions about The Fabulous Five? Quiz each other to see who knows the most Fabulous Facts!

#6 In book #1, *Seventh-Grade Rumors*, why do the other members of the Fabulous Five think Jana is a traitor?

#7 In book #7, *The Kissing Disaster*, why is Melanie worried that the boys she has kissed will get sick?

#8 In book #19, *The Boys-Only Club*, what mystery does Katie uncover in her own backyard?

#9 In book #5, *The Bragging War*, what do the rest of The Fabulous Five make Beth promise at the end of the book?

#10 In book #21, *Jana to the Rescue*, whose name does Melanie accidentally say during the love test?

You can find the answers to these questions, plus five more questions about Fabulous Facts, in the back of The Fabulous Five #27, *The Scapegoat*.

Here are the answers to trivia questions #1–5, which appeared in the back of The Fabulous Five Super #3, *Missing You*.

#1 In The Fabulous Five Super #1, *The Fabulous Five in Trouble*, what unbelievable thing happens to the girls at a sleepover at Katie's house?
The girls each dream about being a different member of The Fabulous Five.

#2 In book #2, *The Trouble with Flirting*, what are the seven tips for flirting that Melanie finds in a magazine?
Make eye contact; act happy and self-confident; use positive body language; give compliments; show genuine interest in the boy; ask him questions; be a good listener.

#3 In book #16, *The Hot-Line Emergency*, whom does Christie suspect of being the mysterious caller?
Jon Smith.

#4 In book #12, *Katie's Dating Tips*, why does the science teacher, Mr. Dracovitch, come to school dressed as Dracula?
To get kids interested in science.

#5 In book #4, *Her Honor, Katie Shannon*, why does Katie get a detention?
For causing a disturbance in class.

ABOUT THE AUTHOR

Betsy Haynes, the daughter of a former news-woman, began scribbling poetry and short stories as soon as she learned to write. A serious writing career, however, had to wait until after her marriage and the arrival of her two children. But that early practice must have paid off, for within three months Mrs. Haynes had sold her first story. In addition to a number of magazine short stories and the Taffy Sinclair series, Mrs. Haynes is also the author of *The Great Mom Swap* and its sequel, *The Great Boyfriend Trap.* She lives in Marco Island, Florida, with her husband, who is also an author.

From Bantam-Skylark Books
IT'S

From Betsy Haynes, the bestselling author of the Taffy Sinclair books, comes THE FABULOUS FIVE. Follow the adventures of Jana Morgan and the rest of THE FABULOUS FIVE in Wakeman Jr. High.

☐	SEVENTH-GRADE RUMORS (Book #1)	15625-X	$2.95
☐	THE TROUBLE WITH FLIRTING (Book #2)	15633-0	$2.95
☐	THE POPULARITY TRAP (Book #3)	15634-9	$2.95
☐	HER HONOR, KATIE SHANNON (Book #4)	15640-3	$2.95
☐	THE BRAGGING WAR (Book #5)	15651-9	$2.75
☐	THE PARENT GAME (Book #6)	15670-5	$2.75
☐	THE KISSING DISASTER (Book #7)	15710-8	$2.75
☐	THE RUNAWAY CRISIS (Book #8)	15719-1	$2.75
☐	THE BOYFRIEND DILEMMA (Book #9)	15720-5	$2.75
☐	PLAYING THE PART (Book #10)	15745-0	$2.75
☐	HIT AND RUN (Book #11)	15746-9	$2.75
☐	KATIE'S DATING TIPS (Book #12)	15748-5	$2.75
☐	THE CHRISTMAS COUNTDOWN (Book #13)	15756-6	$2.75
☐	SEVENTH-GRADE MENACE (Book #14)	15763-9	$2.75
☐	MELANIE'S IDENTITY CRISIS (Book #15)	15775-2	$2.75
☐	THE HOT-LINE EMERGENCY (Book #16)	15781-7	$2.75
☐	CELEBRITY AUCTION (Book #17)	15784-1	$2.75
☐	TEEN TAXI (Book #18)	15794-9	$2.75
☐	THE BOYS-ONLY CLUB (Book #19)	15809-0	$2.95
☐	THE WITCHES OF WAKEMAN (Book #20)	15830-9	$2.75
☐	JANA TO THE RESCUE (Book #21)	15840-6	$2.75
☐	MELANIE'S VALENTINE (Book #22)	15845-7	$2.95
☐	MALL MANIA (Book #23)	15852-X	$2.95
☐	THE GREAT TV TURNOFF (Book #24)	15861-7	$2.95
☐	THE FABULOUS FIVE MINUS ONE (Book #25)	15867-8	$2.95
☐	SUPER EDITION #1 THE FABULOUS FIVE IN TROUBLE	15814-7	$2.95
☐	SUPER EDITION #2 CARIBBEAN ADVENTURE	15831-7	$2.95